Dear Readers,

This time of year, there are plenty of reasons to celebrate—so why not add four spectacular new romances from Bouquet to your list?

Sometimes love turns up even when you're not looking for it. In beloved author Colleen Faulkner's **Taming Ben,** a determined bachelor tries to remember why he objects to relationships when he hires a painter with a heart as big as her smile. Of course, no man can be a **Solitary Man** forever—as the rugged Boston cop in Karen Drogin's emotional offering discovers when his partner's sister shows him why two is better than one.

Next, rising star Suzanne Barrett presents **Hearts At Risk.** When a man who's decided to retreat from the corporate world to his rural family estate finds that a charming woman has a long-term lease on the caretaker's cottage, the first seeds of romance are planted. And last, in **The Littlest Matchmaker** by Laura Phillips, a charming four-year-old is determined to find herself a new mommy, and the manager of the hotel where she and her tycoon father have set up camp is the perfect choice—if only she can convince them to choose love before business. . . .

Enjoy!

Kate Duffy
Editorial Director

A KISS GOOD NIGHT

"I better go," Ben said. "Want me to give Howie a quick walk around the block?"

"Thanks, but I'll do it. I like getting a little air before I go to bed. Helps me sleep."

He pulled his hands out of his pockets, seeming not to quite know what to do. She knew he was thinking about the proverbial good-night kiss. She was thinking about it too.

"Well, good night," he said, surprising her by making no move toward her. In a second, he would turn away.

If he wasn't going to kiss her, she was going to kiss him. Mackenzie leaned toward Ben, and he immediately grabbed her around the waist. He wasn't rough, but he was forceful enough for her to know it wasn't that he hadn't wanted to kiss her, only that he'd wanted to do the right thing.

Mackenzie opened her mouth, reveling in the taste and feel of Ben's lips. A delicious, familiar tightness formed in her belly as he kissed her breathless. She still wanted him, he still wanted her, and there was no doubt about that. . . .

Bachelors Inc:
TAMING
BEN

Colleen Faulkner

ZEBRA BOOKS
Kensington Publishing Corp.
http://www.zebrabooks.com

Prologue

August, 1974

Running down the sidewalk, arms pumping, Ben Gordon glanced over his shoulder. Main Street echoed with the squeal of ten-year-old girls and the pounding of white cotton sneakers. Dang it! He still hadn't lost them.

He raced past Smitty's Hardware and turned the corner. Another block and he would hit the residential area of Land's End, a little town on the eastern shore of the Chesapeake Bay. Ben lived only two blocks from here; if only he could make it home alive. Ben ran harder, his black canvas Keds slapping the hot pavement. If he could just make it to his dad's garden shed where his buddies were waiting for him, he knew he would be safe.

Ben and his friends Owen and Zack had formed a club earlier in the month. They called themselves the GAG Club, as in "girls are gross," and the garden shed was where they held their meetings. If he could just slip into his backyard, even if the girls dared to come to his house, they wouldn't know to look for him in the shed.

Ben glanced over his shoulder again. There were

no girls in tank tops and cut-off shorts in view. Maybe they had given up. Hot and sweaty, he slowed down to a walk to catch his breath. The minute he stopped running, he heard the sounds of their feet again. Behind him, girls came pouring around the corner of the hardware store. Ben took off again.

He ran down the street, across Maple Avenue, and through Mr. Aker's backyard, leaping over a hedge. He didn't know what he'd done to deserve this persecution. He had stopped at the drugstore for a Coke; the place was done up the way it had originally been in the 1950s. While waiting for his soda, he had noticed a couple of girls he knew from school. All he had done was turn around, lean against the countertop, and say hi. Okay, so maybe he was practicing his grin. Girls liked it when he smiled a certain way, and he was getting pretty good at it. Even grown-up women seemed to like it. His mother said his smile was charming. His father said it was trouble.

Just one smile. Then he'd taken his Coke and walked out of the store. He hadn't gotten a block away when he realized the girls were following him. When he started to walk faster, they walked faster. He had tossed his empty can into a garbage bin and taken off. The girls really started to chase him then.

Ben cut across his front lawn, keeping an eye out for any sign of the girls. It looked like he'd lost them. He went through the white picket fence gate and into the backyard. The sprinkler was running, spitting a lazy stream of water over the grass. He

ran through the cold stream and reaching the garden shed, tugged on the door. Locked.

The guys were here.

He knocked furiously. "Let me in! Let me in!"

"Password," came Owen's voice. Owen was new
in town and Ben's current best friend. Ben, Owen,
and Zack were all charter members of the GAG
Club. They'd sworn a holy oath over a moon pie
and warm Orange Crush soda.

Ben banged again irritably. The password had
been his idea, but he hadn't meant that he would
have to use it. It was his garden shed, for Pete's
sake. "Open up, guys! Come on. Hurry!" He
glanced nervously over his shoulder. If the girls
spotted him now, it was all over.

"Password," Zack repeated.

Ben and Zack had been friends since nursery
school. He and his family were what Ben's parents
called hippies. Ben wasn't exactly sure what a hip-
pie was, but as far as he could tell, it meant Zack
could wear cool tie-dyed T-shirts and there was always plenty of food in the house because his mom
bought everything in bulk at a food bank.

Still, dinner at Zack's could be a risky thing.
Sometimes the food was great, like when Mrs. Taylor made grain-fed beefsteaks on the grill and
roasted red potatoes, but those tofu sandwiches she
made were seriously disgusting.

Ben banged on the door of the shed, this time
with a closed fist. "If you two don't let me in, I'm
going to nail you both. *That's* the password!"

He heard the latch lift and he yanked open the
door. "About time," he said, thankful to see his
buddies' dirty faces. "I got a mob scene out here."

Owen stuck his head out the door just before
Ben yanked it shut. "Mob scene? What are you talking about?"

Ben slumped to the floor and leaned against a
wall, taking care not to knock a shovel off one of
the pegs above him. It was hot inside the shed despite the open window in the back, but there was
no way Ben was going outside again. Not until his
mother called him for dinner. He'd rather roast
than be mauled by a bunch of girls. "I was being
chased by these girls from school."

Zack and Owen slid to the plywood floor with a
look on their faces that reflected a mixture of hor-
ror and outright admiration.

"Chasing you? What for?" Owen asked.

Ben rolled his eyes. "I don't know. Why do girls
do any of the things they do?"

His companions nodded in agreement.

"All I did was say hello down at the drugstore.
The next thing I know, they're coming after me."

Zack gave Ben a nudge, sneaker-to-sneaker.
"Well, don't worry now, man; you're safe here."

"Yeah," Owen agreed, giving his new buddy a
reassuring glance. "Just stick with us and you'll be
fine."

One

The Present

Bennett Gordon gripped the wheel of his new Explorer as he spotted a patch of ice on the road up ahead. It was the end of November, early to be this cold on the Chesapeake Bay. They'd had snow last night, less than four inches, but the drifts were high in places. Predictions were calling for a long, hard winter, the coldest in years.

Ben eased through the patchy ice and pushed the accelerator again, anxious to reach his destination. Nothing should be this difficult, he grumbled to himself. He was a general contractor, for heaven's sake. He wasn't supposed to have these kinds of problems.

He had hired an outfit to repaint the living room of his home, a renovated barn here in Land's End. The company was new in town, and he wanted to try them out before using them on one of the jobs he and his partners had lined up. Big mistake. He should have just stuck with Joe Mason and paid his highway robbery prices. At least Joe's boys knew how to paint.

Instead, he'd contacted Sayer and Sons. He'd

never actually spoken to Mackenzie Sayer, the owner, but that was typical. Sayer's receptionist had made the arrangements to send someone out to the house for the estimate. Ben had business that day on another job, so his father, who lived with him, had let Mr. Sayer in and shown him around. Sayer and Sons' bid had come in considerably lower than "Mason's Rip-off Painting," so Ben had thought he had nothing to lose in giving the new guy in town a chance. After all, *he* was a new guy in town, too.

Wrong.

Ben signaled and turned right down a secondary road. The fields on both sides of him were white and frosty and uneven with drifting snow; cut cornstalks stuck up like stalagmites. It was a desolate area, which made it all the more beautiful on this snowy morning. Out at the end of this road, on the edge of the bay, there was an old plantation home. That was where Mackenzie Sayer's receptionist said Ben could find him. That was where Mr. Sayer was going to get a piece of Ben's mind.

Sayer and Sons had sent their painters out, all right. They'd arrived on time and gotten right to work. They had prepped the walls and taped over woodwork to protect it. Then the painters started painting, and that was when they got into trouble. It was the worst paint job Ben had ever seen in his life. His buddy Zack's ten-year-old could have done a better job.

The paint was too thin in some places, too thick in others. There were spatters of paint on the ceiling, which had not needed painting, and they had actually painted over some of the electrical outlets.

Yesterday after lunch, he had mentioned the problems to one of the painters. Ben could have sworn the guy smelled of whiskey, but he couldn't be sure. The workmen had promised they would clean up and be more careful in the future. They hadn't cleaned up, and they were still painting over electrical sockets. This morning had been the last straw, though. Ben had gone to open a living room window to let in a little cold air and discovered it was painted shut.

He had called Mr. Sayer right away, but the man hadn't been in. Now Ben was tracking him down personally. He'd make this right or he would never paint another house in Land's End again. Ben would see to that.

As Ben rounded a curve, he spotted a red sports car pulled off to the side of the road. An old Porche. Very nice. A woman leaned into the trunk.

Even nicer. She was clad in jeans with legs that seemed to reach to the sky, and what a bottom. She was wearing a lime-green down coat, her long, blond hair blowing in the wind. The scene looked like one of those car commercials on TV that ran during sports events: a beautiful woman, a sweet sports car.

Ben hit his brakes as he passed the Porche and the blonde. He would have stopped to help anyone on such a lonely road, but he had to confess, this woman intrigued him. He'd always been a sucker for good-looking women in distress.

He didn't put down the passenger window to ask if she needed help. He just backed up and pulled in behind her, then put on his flashers in case someone else came around the curve.

The woman raised her head, a jack in her hand. Sweet Mary, she was almost as tall as he was. An Amazon!

She turned to look at him.

An Amazon, and not just beautiful, but drop-dead ravishing to boot.

"Hey there. Need some help?" He slipped his hands into his leather gloves, keeping his tone casual. Playing it cool.

She stared at him for a second, almost as if she knew him, but then her face changed. She lit up with the most intriguing half smile, half grin. It was downright sexy.

"It's the new millennium. Women can change tires," she deadpanned. "But sure, some help would be nice."

He took the jack from her and offered his right hand. "Bennett Gordon."

She took his hand slowly in her slender one, and he was mesmerized. She was even more beautiful close up. He hoped he wasn't drooling. Maybe she wasn't in a car commercial, after all. Maybe it was one of those romantic love-at-first-sight coffee commercials.

Ben had never believed in love at first sight. He wasn't even certain he believed in love, but this woman gave his heart a hard tug.

"Nice to meet you, Bennett Gordon." She said it with a silky deep voice that shot warmth through him, despite the freezing temperatures.

To his dismay, she didn't give him her name, but that was understandable. They were out on a lonely country road, and he realized that these days women needed to be careful with strangers. Even harmless clean-cut looking ones like himself.

He made himself move to the flat. If he stood here ogling her for too long, he might scare her. Then he'd never get her name and number out of her. "Got a tire iron?"

She was one step ahead of him. She pulled a tire iron from the trunk and passed it like a nurse assisting a doctor in an operating room. She had a strange look on her face, one that made him a little uncomfortable. Was she laughing at him? He hadn't had anything to eat so he couldn't have food on his chin.

But she was still amazingly gorgeous, even with that amused look on her face.

As Ben jacked up the car to a safe height, he wondered if this could be a joke. Was that what was funny? Did his buddies Owen and Zack send this woman out on this road to tempt him?

Months ago the three of them had set around a table at a pizza place in town and formed their house-restoration business. At the same time, they had all agreed to give up dating women. They'd all suffered through bad relationships and were tired of it. They had named their company Land's End Renovations, but their corporation was Bachelors Incorporated.

Ben was the only one who had taken the idea seriously. Owen and Zack were both recently married— Owen to his ex-wife, no less. But Ben wasn't looking for anything so permanent, and he'd had enough brief, shallow relationships. He'd had enough of sleeping with women only to wake up in the morning to wish he hadn't. He didn't need a woman to stroke his ego. He had a good business, his dad, and the best friends a man could ask for.

Ben eyed the blonde. No, this couldn't be a prank. Too difficult to set up.

He pulled the flat tire off the axle and rolled it to the trunk as she rolled the spare past him. She was a take-charge kind of woman and he admired that. Most of the women he knew would have leaned against the trunk and filed their nails while he froze his butt off changing her tire.

The blonde lifted the spare and placed it on the axle. He tossed the flat into her trunk and went back to the mounted spare. She was already putting the lug nuts back on. He handed the others to her, admiring the way she spun the tire iron. Definitely a confident lady.

He didn't know that he had ever met anyone who had piqued his interest like this woman did.

He watched as she tightened the last nut. "Want me to give them another turn, just to be sure they're secure enough?" he asked, pointing.

"Nah. I think they're fine." She smiled, returning the jack and tire iron to the trunk and slamming it shut. "Thanks for your help, Bennett Gordon." She walked around the car and climbed in. "Have a nice day!"

Ben stood there like a bumpkin, his cold hands stuffed in his pockets as he watched her pull away.

When she disappeared around the next curve, he jumped back into his SUV and started it up. He blasted the heat on high. He hadn't been outside long, but his toes were tingling.

He shook his head, disgusted with himself. Bachelors Inc. be damned, why hadn't he gotten her name or phone number? Too enthralled. Maybe just a little intimidated. It took a lot of woman to intimidate Ben, but the mysterious blonde had been a lot of woman—more woman than he'd ever seen. And she hadn't acted as if she was interested in him. That intrigued him, too. Most women liked him right away. Crazy over him. Zack and Owen called him a lady magnet.

He pulled off his gloves and rubbed his hands together for warmth in front of one of the vents, wondering how he could track her down. He had no name, no information, except that she was a six-foot blonde in a red '69ish Porche.

Shoot, if she was on this back road, she had to live around Land's End, didn't she? But she had to be new in town. He'd have to do some asking around.

When his hands were warm, he put the car in gear and eased it back onto the road. In five minutes, he reached the old plantation house where Mack Sayer was supposed to be checking on a job. Irritably, Ben wondered why Sayer hadn't come by to check the job at his house. If he had, maybe Ben's windows wouldn't be painted shut right now.

Sure enough, there was an older panel van with the words *Sayer and Sons* freshly painted on the side. As he pulled into a little parking area, he was surprised to see the red sports car there, too.

He had heard new people had bought the old Conley Plantation. Could the blonde have bought this mansion? She looked too young to have this kind of money. But who knew with the stock market these days? Of course, if this *was* her home, that presented a new problem. Should he just walk up and bang on the door looking for this Sayer guy? What if the blonde answered the door? Would she think he was following her? Should he go home and wait for Sayer to call him back?

But then Ben thought about the mess his house was in and grew angry all over again. He'd just knock on the door and take it from there. He wasn't cutting Mr. Sayer any slack just because he might be working for the beautiful Amazon.

Ben marched up to the front door, which was open. Now he didn't have to worry about knocking. The blonde was nowhere to be seen. Two men in white coveralls were on ladders, painting just inside the door in the wainscoted hallway.

"Morning," Ben said. "I'm looking for Mackenzie Sayer. His receptionist said I could find him on this job."

He summed the two men up. One looked old enough to have sons in the business. Could be him. The other man looked as if he was barely out of high school.

"Who'd you say you were?" the older man asked, paint brush poised.

Must not be Mackenzie, else he'd have fessed up by now. "My name's Bennett Gordon."

"And you want the boss . . . why?"

Ben grew more irritated. He had work of his own to do today; he didn't have time for this. "I'm a client. An *unhappy* client," he emphasized. He could feel himself growing hot around the collar of his wool sweater. "Look, just point me in the right direction of your boss and I'll be on my way."

Ben heard footsteps and glanced up to see the blonde come from a room that looked like a library. Sheets covered the furniture. She was smiling that knock-'em-dead smile of hers.

Ben smiled back. "Sorry to bother you." He chuckled. "Seems we were headed for the same place. I'm looking for Mr. Mackenzie Sayer, the painter."

The blonde glanced at the two men on the ladders who were looking at her wide-eyed.

It only took Ben a second to realize he'd made a mistake. An idiotic mistake. He had never actually spoken to the owner of the painting business. No one had said Mackenzie Sayer was a man. The Amazon was Mackenzie Sayer. He could have smacked himself on the forehead. He'd been in the contracting business long enough to know never to make assumptions.

The blonde took her time walking over. The smile was gone. Now she had *her* business face on.

"Mackenzie Sayer?" he asked.

She nodded.

He gave a little laugh, not as confident as the last. "I'm sorry. I apologize. I assumed—"

"I was a man." She wasn't laughing.

"Well, the sign did said Sayer and Sons," he defended. "Around here, ordinarily, businesses like this are a father and son, not a wom—" He was backing himself against a wall, poised to stuff his other foot in his mouth. He looked up at her—no, not up—straight into her eyes. "There is no father, no sons, are there?" he asked.

She shook her head. Still no smile.

He tried a handsome, boyish grin. It always worked. "I do apologize."

It didn't work.

"You came here for a reason other than to verify my gender, Mr. Gordon?" she asked coolly.

The two painters, who had been gawking, suddenly concentrated on loading their brushes.

"Um, yes." He motioned, stalling to get his mind straight. He couldn't believe this woman was the man he was pissed with. He couldn't believe he'd made this big a fool of himself in front of a woman he wanted to ask out. "Can we talk outside?"

She motioned to the door and they stepped out. She waited.

He glanced out over the snowy grounds, then at her. There was a stone fountain in the side yard, cold and dry now. "You're doing a job for me."

She folded her arms over her chest, surprised. "I am?"

"Yeah, out on Cinder Road."

She lowered his gaze, thinking. She shook her head. "Cinder Road, Cinder Road." She looked up, making the connection. "The converted barn."

He nodded. "That's mine."

She frowned, her forehead creasing. "But an elderly man hired me. A Max Gordon."

"That's right. My dad. He lives with me. I was out on a job, so he met with you."

He could have sworn she cursed under her breath. She looked away, then back at him. "Okay, so what's the problem? Why did you come to one of my sites?"

"I came because the men you have working for you are imbeciles."

She flinched.

"They've got paint on the ceiling, paint on receptacles and now they've painted a window closed." He gained momentum. "I wouldn't be surprised if they've painted my damned cat."

Not even a twitch of a smile. "I'll have to come out and take a look," she snapped.

She was angry with him, and he wasn't sure why. It was her employees who had screwed up. He had a right to be angry. Of course, he had jumped the gun and tracked her down on another job instead of waiting for her to call him back. He paused. "Look, I shouldn't have come out here. I should have sent the painters packing and waited for you to return my call."

She held his gaze. He liked this, looking right into her green eyes.

She glanced down. For the first time, he realized she was wearing work boots similar to his. They were paint-spattered.

She flipped her hair over her shoulder. "Let me talk to my guys here and then I'll come out."

"Great." It was very cold out and he wished he hadn't left his gloves in the car. He jammed his hands into his coat pockets. "Then I'll just go back to the house and wait for you."

She nodded and walked inside without another word.

Mackenzie climbed into her car and banged her fist on the steering wheel. Damn, she thought. She knew it was dangerous coming back to her old hometown to start her new business. She knew that eventually she would run into old classmates from school.

But Bennett Gordon? She hadn't fathomed he

would be here. Last she had heard, he was some-where up north, a big-shot contractor out of Philly.

She cranked hard on the engine, not giving the car the respect the old broad deserved. She slammed it into gear and left the driveway faster than she should have, the rear tires sliding on the icy drive. Mackenzie felt her eyes burning in their sockets.

Of all the ghosts in her closet to haunt her now. *Bennett Gordon.* Bennett Gordon, captain of the soc-cer team, homecoming king, president of his senior class the year she was a junior.

He had broken her heart twenty years ago, and the jerk didn't even remember her.

Two

Mackenzie gripped the steering wheel. Talk about bad luck; she should never have gotten out of bed this morning. First Bennett Gordon, the object of her unrequited love for a zillion years, stops to help her with the flat. She was shocked by his sudden appearance, so relieved that he didn't recognize her that she'd acted like a goose. Once the tire was fixed she thought she could make her getaway and never see him again.

Ten minutes later he shows up at one of her work sites looking for her. Mackenzie groaned aloud. She couldn't believe Bennett had hired her company to paint his house. She couldn't believe she hadn't made the connection when she saw the last name. But why would she? There were probably twenty Gordons in the Land's End phone book. Who would have ever thought that like her, Ben had come back to his hometown? Then, when she met the charming elderly man at the site, he'd acted as if it was his home. No mention of Ben was made.

Mackenzie took a deep breath and turned up the heat in the car. She knew she was reacting badly. There was no need for her to be this disturbed. High school was a long time ago. Whatever Ben did to her, however she felt about him, shouldn't interfere with business. She couldn't let it interfere.

She knew what she had to do. She would go to Bennett's house, hear his complaint, check out the work, and then solve the problem. It was probably nothing; a little paint on the windowpane or something equally trivial. Nothing a swipe with a rag dipped in mineral spirits couldn't solve. Bennett Gordon didn't have to be a problem if she didn't let him become one.

That he didn't recognize her should make it easier. That it wasn't easier was another aggravation she didn't need.

Her brain told her to be logical and calm as she turned onto the main road heading back into Land's End. But inside, her heart was fighting logic tooth and nail. Just seeing Ben jump out of that SUV as if he were some kind of superhero had made her heart trip and fall at the same time.

He was even more handsome than she remembered. A mature handsome. Ben wasn't pretty like the male models of the day, but had classic good looks with his slightly wavy, dark hair cut short and intriguing blue eyes.

He was more handsome, and she'd probably been even more unattractive in high school than she remembered, she thought morosely.

Mackenzie sighed, thinking back, not wanting to, but unable to bury the memories any longer. She had never known her father, who abandoned her mother when she was pregnant. After her mother died of cancer when Mackenzie was in grade school, she had moved in with her maternal grandmother. The old-world German woman had never meant to be unkind, but she had not understood the world Mackenzie was growing up in. She hadn't understood the importance of wearing the right jeans or having a TV so Mackenzie could keep up with all the cool shows. Her grandmother hadn't understood that all that strudel and the rich pancakes that tasted so good made Mackenzie so miserable.

To Grandmother Frieda, food was everything. Food meant happiness, contentment, and so to please her grandmother, she had eaten. And eaten. And eaten. In elementary school, when she still went by Margaret, her given name, rather than her middle name, which she switched to in college, the kids had called her "Mega-Margaret," or just "Mega." In high school, they had apparently learned enough manners not to call her names, but the punishment there had been worse. In high school she was nearly invisible to all but a few friends who were also misfits in one way or another.

Just thinking about those years brought an ache to Mackenzie's chest, not just for herself, but for the others. They had all suffered as social outcasts because they were different. She couldn't recall that anyone was mean to her or her friends; they were just nonentities. And in a way, that was just as cruel as the name-calling. At least to be ridiculed was to have one's existence acknowledged.

Somehow, Mackenzie had survived high school. She had gone off to college and somewhere in those lean years, she had grown a little taller still and shed the weight. She transformed, not overnight, but slowly as if evolving through the stages of a moth. And finally—she caught a glimpse of

herself in the rearview mirror—finally, she had
woken up one morning to realize she was beautiful.
That was when she started going by her middle
name, which she felt better suited her personality.
People smiled at her on the streets. Men she didn't
know asked her to dance in bars when she went
out with girlfriends. She was never without a date
on a Friday or a Saturday night.

But being tall and beautiful did not come without
consequences. Mackenzie learned that single
women wanted to be friendly with her because she
was a guy magnet. Women who were married or
dating one man exclusively didn't want her for a
friend for fear she would steal theirs. Men wanted
to date her so that they could show up at restau-
rants with a striking beauty on their arm. It was as
lonely a life as the one she had experienced in
Land's End.

Mackenzie signaled and pulled in behind Ben's
SUV. It was a nice house. Originally, it had been
an eighteenth-century barn, Ben's father had explained when she came out to give her estimate for
the painting. The renovations had been done with
taste and appreciation for the original state of the
brick structure. As an artist, Mackenzie could appreciate such a home. When she had come to give
the estimate, she had even fantasized that once her
business got off the ground, she might even be able
to tackle a job like this and renovate her own old
place. It sure would beat the two-bedroom apartment off the supermarket parking lot she was living
in now.

Mackenzie cut the engine and slipped her gloves
on, stalling for time. Did she just come out and tell

Bennett who she was? Ask him if he remembered her? But why should she? The ass. He had barely spoken to her in high school, though she was in two of his classes his senior year. Now that she was tall, had lost a few pounds, and had discovered the joys of highlighting and contacts, suddenly he was Mr. Flirtatious.

She ground her teeth and climbed out of her car, slamming the door. It wasn't good for the car, but it made her feel better. As she trudged through a snowdrift, she passed another paneled truck painted with her company's emblem on it.

Ben met her at the side door. "Thanks for coming right over," he said. He was almost friendly now, bordering on sheepish. "I've got a job I need to get out to, so I appreciate your promptness."

He held open the door for her. She let him. "What kind of business do you have?"

"My buddies and I do renovations and restoration of old houses. I'm the general contractor."

They were in a mudroom. He had left the original inside panels of the old barn exposed in the room, though insulation had been added, she was sure. It was toasty warm inside. Last time she had been here, Mr. Gordon had let her in the front so she hadn't seen this charming room.

She slipped out of her coat. "So you and your friends run the company?" she asked, trying not to sound too interested.

He nodded. "We went into business together this summer. Owen Thomas is an architect; Zack Taylor's a cabinetmaker. I do the general contracting."

She stared at him in amazement, though why she was surprised, she didn't know. The three had been best friends for as long as she'd known them. It was just that they had all separated after high school, gone to different colleges. She knew Zack and Owen had both married; hell, Owen had married his grammar-school sweetheart. She had never heard about Ben other than his work in Philly. She glanced at his left hand, no ring, but what did that mean these days? Of course he had been flirtatious with her when he'd helped her change her tire, but that didn't mean anything these days either. Mackenzie knew that all too well.

"To be honest with you," Ben said. "That was why I called your company. I wanted to see what kind of work you did. We're looking for some more painters."

Great. Ben—the last man on earth she'd wanted to run into—wasn't happy with the painters she'd sent out and he was in a position to really screw up her fledgling business. Something told Mackenzie that his complaint was more than a few paint splatters. Could the day possibly become any worse?

"Can I take your coat?" he asked.

She shook her head and draped it over her arm. She wanted to get out of here as quickly as possible. Ben was a charmer, just like he'd been in high school. Way too charming.

"So what's your complaint, Bennett?" She stepped into the living area that stretched two stories overhead with a loft and balcony on the second floor. The open ceiling and bare trusses had taken her breath away the first time she had seen the room. It was also a painting company's dream. She needed this job.

"My complaint"—he crossed the room, which

had to be twenty-five feet wide, to the window—"is that my windows won't open." He demonstrated.

She rolled her eyes, making no attempt not to sound patronizing. A part of her hated this man, hated him for how he had once made her feel. "In weather like this, after they've been painted, they sometimes stick." She walked over, made sure the window was unlocked and gave it a push.

He crossed his arms over his broad chest and waited impatiently.

It wasn't until she gave the window a second shove that she saw that the window was, indeed, painted shut. Shoot, she thought.

Next he gestured to an electrical socket below the windowsill, looking a little bit like a game-show model showing off curtain number two. The cover had been removed, as it was supposed to have been, but the painter had been so careless that he had rolled right over the actual sockets. They would have to be replaced or removed and carefully scraped.

Double shoot.

Ben pointed to the hardwood floor. The wide, wormholed boards were splattered with the "warm ecru" she had purchased for the job. And it wasn't just a few dots either, there were drops of hardened paint on the old floor that were the size of quarters and half dollars.

Mackenzie could feel a headache coming on. A bad one. "I'm terribly sorry," she said, using her business voice. This was all she needed right now. With the monthly loan payments on the vehicles and equipment and the payroll, she couldn't afford to lose the job. "I'll get this cleaned up and get the job done right, I promise you."

He appeared doubtful.

"My truck's still out front. Where are my employees?"

He pointed in the opposite direction they had come. "My back deck. Lunch."

She glanced at her wristwatch. It was 11:20. "Lunch?"

"Actually, I think it's prelunch, which comes about an hour and a half after the coffee and doughnut break. They have lunch about one, then another break at three, according to my dad. He's taken to calling it their high tea."

It was all Mackenzie could do to keep from moaning out loud. No wonder the damned job was taking so long. She glanced in the direction Ben had pointed. "Do you mind?"

He opened his arms. "Not in the least." He spoke so graciously that it was annoying. "Straight through into the kitchen. The deck is out the side door."

Mackenzie strode through the living room, into the kitchen, and out the door. She found her crew—Gary, Sam, and Louie—lounging on plastic deck chairs. They looked like the Three Stooges lined up in their chairs. When she stepped out onto the deck, Gary, the crew leader, jumped to his feet.

"Boss."

His nose was red, his face flushed. It was cold out, but not *that* cold.

"Gary, Mr. Gordon called me about this job. He's not happy."

"He's not happy?" Gary brushed his longish needed-a-wash hair out of his eyes.

Was he slurring?

She glanced at the other two. They were red-faced, too.

"He said he spoke to you more than once about your sloppiness."

"Oh, boss. A couple drips here and there. 'Tweren't no big deal. Nothin' that can't be fixed." He worked the zipper of his white coveralls, avoiding eye contact.

"Nothin' that can't be fixed," Louie echoed.

Mackenzie took a step closer to Gary. "You should have told me that Mr. Gordon had a problem with your work, Gary. I don't appreciate having a client have to tell me."

"Aw, boss. He's just too damned picky is all." Gary swiped at the air.

Mackenzie caught a whiff of his breath. The experienced painters she had hired were drinking on the job? No wonder they had painted the damned window shut!

"Gary," she glanced at the other two, "have you guys been drinking?"

They all suddenly appeared frozen in time.

She grabbed the insulated thermos off the picnic table and took a whiff.

"C-coffee," Gary stammered.

It was coffee all right and something stronger. Whiskey.

Mackenzie cursed under her breath. She didn't curse often, but today was turning out to be a doozy of a day.

This was all she needed. Experienced painters

weren't easy to come by. Experienced painters who didn't drink on the job were apparently even more difficult to find.

She rubbed her temple where the headache was starting. "You guys are fired."

The other two stooges shot up out of their deck chairs.

"What?"

"Fired?"

"Come on, boss," Gary slurred. "It's cold. Just a little nip to keep the blood circulating."

"Fired. Return the van to the office. Ellie will cut your checks. I'll call ahead." She pushed through the door, back into the kitchen.

"But, boss—"

She slammed the door shut.

Ben was standing there. "They've been drinking," she said, staring at the hardwood floor. The kitchen was very pretty, not as masculine as she would have expected for a home with two men living alone. "But then I guess you already knew that."

"Good help isn't easy to find."

It was nice of him to say that, but right this minute, she wasn't in the mood for his sympathy. She passed him, headed for the living room. All she wanted to do was get out of here right now. "Look, I'm very sorry about this. Someone will be here tomorrow morning to get this mess cleaned up and start repainting."

"Good enough."

She glanced at him as she zipped up her coat. "I appreciate your understanding. I guarantee it will be done right if I have to do it myself. And I'll give you a ten percent discount." The discount would cut her profits, especially since she would have to purchase more paint, but this man was a contractor. He could bring her more work. It had to be done.

She barely glanced at Ben. "I can let myself out," she said coolly as she hurried out through the mudroom, closing the door hard behind her, not giving him a chance to follow. She trudged through the icy snow, and climbed into her car.

How was she going to make good on her promise and find another crew by morning? She couldn't pull the guys off the Conley place to work this job. Her other crew was painting apartments in a new complex in town. She couldn't pull them off either. Her payment depended on getting done on time.

Mackenzie slid her car into gear and hit the gas. The tires spun.

She pushed it into first and inched ahead a little bit, then reversed again. The sports car rocked and the tires spun again. For a good five minutes she rocked the car back and forth hoping by some miracle that she would break free and be able to get out of here. That, or at least maybe the guys would come out and give her a push.

But eventually she realized she was just making the rut worse, and the guys were not coming. They were probably finishing up their coffee on the deck. No need to hurry now.

Mackenzie stomped across the snow to Bennett's back door. She'd have almost rather walked back to the office than had to do this. She rang the doorbell.

Ben opened the door. He was grinning. "Little

problem?" He must have been watching from the mudroom window because he was already putting his coat on.

She sighed audibly. "Could you give me a push, a pull, or something with your Explorer. I would ask my ex-crew, but considering their state of inebriation, they might hurt themselves."

"Sure, I can help." Handsome smile. "Just one thing."

She lifted an eyebrow. She wasn't giving him more than a ten percent discount. He could forget that. "Yes?"

"Go out to dinner with me."

Three

Mackenzie stared at Ben. A date? He was asking her out on a date?

After what he did to her? After the way he had humiliated her?

Okay, so maybe it had been twenty years ago or so, and maybe he didn't realize who she was. But that didn't change the facts.

He waited, that goofy grin on his face.

The same grin that had attracted her to him all those years ago. The same grin that, though she hated to admit it, still made her go soft inside.

Mackenzie didn't know why she was surprised he asked her out. He had flirted back on the roadside, though she had to give him credit, it had been covert flirting. And she was an attractive, eligible woman well beyond the age of consent. And he was . . . well, he was a man. Unattached, apparently. So why was she surprised?

Because a small part of her was still that overweight, mousy-haired, thick-lensed girl she had been. A small part of her could not believe Bennett Gordon would be interested in Margaret Mackenzie Sayer.

She met his gaze, angry. Hurting inside. "Forget

it!" She spun around and tramped off through the snow. "I'll walk."

Ben ran after her. "Hey, wait!"

She could hear him struggling to put on his coat as he followed her through the snowdrifts outside the house. "I'm kidding. Wait!"

She spun back around, her jaw set in anger. "You're kidding about being willing to help me out of the snow in exchange for a date, or you're kidding about wanting to go out with me at all?"

Ben halted, fastening his jacket. He stared at her for a minute, as if confused. "Listen, I was kidding. A joke. You know, I was being humorous, trying to get you to go out with me by being funny."

She stared, unamused.

He lifted his hands, palms out in surrender. "I didn't mean to offend you. I'll get you out of here." He exhaled. "Jeez, a little touchy there, aren't you? I mean it's not an insult, Mackenzie, a man asking you out to dinner."

Mackenzie. She liked the way he said her name.

She lowered her gaze to her boots, covered with snow. He was right. She had overreacted, and she felt silly.

Did he *still* not remember who she was?

Obviously not.

"Could you just help me get my car out?" she asked evenly. "I've got a lot of work to do."

"Sure." He sounded as if he were going to say something else, but then he just exhaled and turned back toward his car.

With the help of a towrope and his SUV, Ben had Mackenzie's car out in a matter of minutes. He turned it around in the driveway, pulled it out of the drift, and left it at the end of the drive facing the road.

"I left it running," he said, unfolding his long legs as he climbed out of her car. "It should be warm inside."

That was nice of him to think of her comfort. Very nice. Most of the men she had dated over the years had been too concerned about themselves to think of anyone else. Of course, if the man had shoveled his driveway properly, she wouldn't have gotten stuck in the first place. "Someone will be here in the morning," she repeated.

Mackenzie got back in her car, shifted into gear and touched the gas lightly. She eased out of Ben's driveway and down the road, wishing she'd never come back to Land's End.

"Pop?" Ben stirred the fresh green beans he was sautéing.

"Upstairs," Max Gordon called from elsewhere in the house.

"Dinner's just about ready." He added a little more butter to the green beans. He had Monterey chicken and red-skinned potatoes baking in the oven.

"Coming."

A minute later seventy-seven-year-old Max appeared in the doorway, his silver hair damp and combed off to one side the way it was for every meal. Ben guessed it was a throwback from his childhood in the thirties.

"I caught up with Sayer today," he told his father

casually as he added a little fresh minced garlic to the beans.

"That right?" Max began to set the table in the large eat-in kitchen.

Ben hadn't included a dining room in the floor plan when he'd restored the barn. No need for that in a man's house, just wasted space that would have to be dusted.

"She going to make good on the work?"

Ben stopped scooping green beans onto one of the dinner plates on the Corian counter and looked at his dad. "You knew Mackenzie Sayer was a she," he said with accusation.

"I may be old, my memory might come and go a bit, but there's no missing that one was female. All ten feet of her." Max grinned as he placed a napkin under both forks.

Ben waved the serving spoon. "Well, why didn't you tell me that a woman owned the business?"

Max stared at his son. "You made the arrangements, I was just meeting her at the door." He frowned. " 'Sides, why would you care if Mackenzie Sayer was a he, a she, or a hippo, so long as the painting got done?" He studied his son. "You gone male chauvinist on me, boy, because you know, I taught you better than that. Your mama taught you better."

Ben turned his back on his father to dole out the rest of the beans on the other plate. "I don't care if Mackenzie Sayer is a man or a woman. I was just surprised."

"Didn't make a fool of yourself, did you, son?"

When Ben didn't answer right away, Max cackled.

"Did, didn't you? You thought that long-legged she-colt was a he and went after *him* with an attitude."

Ben slipped on a hot mitt and pulled the chicken and potatoes out of the oven. He and his dad took turns cooking when they were both home. His dad made old-fashioned meals like beef stew and chicken à la king. It reminded Ben of his happy childhood and of his mother so he didn't mind, but he preferred meals with more of a gourmet touch. He was always experimenting in the kitchen. "I think I had a right to a little attitude. The damned window is painted shut." He gestured indignantly.

Max went on cackling. "Gave you a run for your money, did she?"

Ben carried the plates to the table and they sat down. Max said grace and crossed himself. Another throwback from his childhood days. He never missed Sunday Mass either.

Ben picked up his fork, mulling over the day. There was something about Mackenzie that he couldn't put his finger on. Something about the way she had spoken to him—almost as if she knew him, or thought she did. Ben pushed a forkful of beans into his mouth. They were al dente just the way he liked them and all buttery and garlicky. "Dad, when Mackenzie was here did she say anything about herself?"

Max shook the salt shaker over everything on his plate. It made Ben crazy. He went to all this trouble to make his father a nice meal, and then Max covered it with salt. Ben guessed he ought to be relieved Max wasn't putting ketchup on everything as well.

"Nope, didn't say anything except that her outfit had only been around a few months."

Ben nodded. He knew he'd never met her before. He wouldn't forget a face like hers or that she was almost as tall as he was, but still, he couldn't shake this weird feeling that somehow he knew her. Maybe he'd talked to her on the phone about a job or something and just didn't remember. He'd have to ask Zack and Owen if they recalled her name.

"Why do you ask?" Max wiped his mouth with his napkin and dove into the potatoes.

"I don't know. She just acted a little oddly."

Max pointed at his son with his fork. "You try to put a move on her?" He sounded hopeful.

Ben frowned. "Pop."

"Nice lookin' gal. Smart, too."

"She's tall, an Amazon," Ben muttered.

"That intimidate you, son? A woman as tall as you?"

Ben glanced up. "She isn't as tall as I am." He looked at his plate again. "And no, that doesn't intimidate me."

Max gave a snort as he sliced off a piece of chicken. "All those other gals you went with, at least the ones I met, were all little itty-bitty things. Brisk wind and they'd blow right off the street."

"I'm not marrying her, Dad." Ben tried to be patient. "Just having her paint my living room."

"Could, you know," Max said thoughtfully.

"Could what? Marry her?" The conversation was getting ridiculous now. "Pop, I'm not marrying the painter." He pushed aside the thought that she did interest him, that he'd actually asked her out. It had been a moment of weakness. Nothing more.

"Of course you're not marrying her." Max slammed down his fork. "Not at least without dating first."

Ben groaned. "I'm not dating the painter or anyone else. I'm just getting my living room painted."

"Big mistake. Big mistake," Max mouthed.

Ben was losing his appetite. He loved his father dearly and was glad to be able to share a home with him, but sometimes the old man made him crazy. "We're not going to have this conversation."

"I just think you ought to try dating again. Only this time, don't be picking women up in bars and at parties where they serve raw fish and call it food."

"Pop—"

"Look at Owen and Zack. Found themselves good women, both of them. Happier than pigs in mud."

Ben set down his fork. They'd had this conversation twice since Zack's wedding Saturday. "Pop, please."

"Your mother, best thing that ever happened to me. Best years of my life, God rest her soul." Max crossed himself, his fork still in his hand.

Ben knew better than to argue with his father once he began talking about his mother. It was a losing battle.

After Ben's mother died a few years ago and Max had gotten through his mourning period, he'd begun dating. Actively. He said he needed a woman to love and was determined to find another wife. Ben conjectured that Max had dated just about every single woman between the ages of sixty and eighty at the Land's End Senior Center. Now he was spreading out to neighboring towns. And it wasn't enough that this was his personal crusade, now Max wanted his son to follow in his footsteps.

"You find yourself a good woman and you'll be a happy man, Bennett."

Now he was calling him Bennett.

"Mark my words. You'll be a happy man and then I'll die peacefully."

"I am a happy man." Ben got up with his plate without finishing his meal. "I'm perfectly content with the life I have. And you're not dying."

"We all die, son. We're born dying."

"Not anytime soon, you're not dying."

Max ignored him. "I understand how you feel, but you just think you're content because you don't know any better."

Ben went to the counter and pulled plastic wrap out of the drawer to cover his plate. He'd eat his dinner in peace later. "You going out tonight, Pop?"

"Bingo at the senior center. Seven thirty."

"Need a ride?"

"Nope." He scraped his plate nosily. "Myrtle the Turtle's coming by for me."

Myrtle was his latest flame. Seventy-two and still worked three days a week for a lumber company. They'd been dating a week.

"Well, I'm going to get some work done in my office." He pushed his covered plate into the fridge. "Behave yourself and have a good time."

Max winked as Ben left the kitchen. "Always do, son. Always do."

* * *

Mackenzie walked down the hall that smelled of disinfectant, medications and dying. She hated that cloying smell. And no matter how cheery the wallpaper was or how big the picture windows that showed a view of the manicured lawns were, it was the smell of places like this that embedded in your mind.

"Evening, Laura." Mackenzie passed the nursing station.

A young black woman glanced up and smiled. "Hey, Mackenzie."

"How was she today?"

Laura smiled kindly. "About the same. Didn't eat much for supper. You know she likes you to be here for supper."

"Maybe I can get her to eat a little snack."

"You know where to find it." Laura turned back to the paperwork on the desk in front of her.

"Have a nice evening," Mackenzie said with a wave.

"You, too, hon."

Mackenzie passed several rooms and then turned into one with Sayer labeled on the door. Despite how tired she was and what a lousy day she'd had, she put on a smile. You just never know, the nurses had told her. These patients sometimes see and know more than we realize.

"Hi there, Nana." Mackenzie walked into the bright room with its blue wallpaper and yellow curtains. "How are you, sweetie?"

Mackenzie went to the hospital bed and leaned over her grandmother and kissed her wrinkled forehead. She smelled of Ivory soap and fabric softener, but there was still that smell of old age that clung to her paper-thin skin.

Her grandmother's eyes were open, but she neither spoke nor looked at Mackenzie. She never did. Not since the last stroke five months ago.

"I brought the newspaper. I thought I could read to you for a while." Mackenzie pulled up an upholstered chair she had brought from her grandmother's home before she sold it. It had been one of her grandmother's favorite pieces of furniture. Mackenzie had brought a few other pieces as well. Though the room was small, the staff had encouraged her to bring items that were familiar to her grandmother. It made the transition from home to a care facility easier, they had explained during the admission process.

So Mackenzie had brought the chair and a nightstand to go beside her grandmother's bed. She had brought an old, sturdy rosewood dresser and a lamp, as well as some personal items. She had also brought photos and made a small gallery on the wall directly across from Nana's bed. There were pictures of her husband, of her wedding day, and of her two children, now deceased, as well as photos of Mackenzie when she was little. On the other walls, Mackenzie had hung some of her paintings. The room was cozy, but it still wasn't home.

Mackenzie tossed her coat on the end of the bed, sat down, and spread the newspaper on her lap. "We'll read a little and then maybe we'll have a snack. Laura says she saved us some Jell-O. You know how much I like Jell-O." She patted her grandmother's hand.

There was no response. There never was.

Mackenzie started to read aloud an article from the front page of the paper. It was about the change in migration of the local waterfowl. Ordinarily she would have been interested. One of her favorite things to paint was the local landscape with wildlife.

She read two paragraphs aloud and stopped. She couldn't concentrate and she kept losing her place. "Okay," she said, as she glanced at another headline. "Listen to this. More welfare reform on the way. Did you know the state is working on a dental program for children of low-income families?" She scanned the article and then folded the paper with a sigh.

"Nah," she said. "I don't feel much like reading the paper tonight either." She leaned forward and rubbed her grandmother's hand. It was cool to the touch.

Nana stared at the pictures on the wall. Or maybe at the light fixture on the ceiling. She rarely blinked.

"I ran into a snag with the business today," Mackenzie said, sliding back in her chair. "Not a big deal, but the timing couldn't be worse. I had to fire one of my crews. The whole crew!" She stared at the smooth blankets that covered her grandmother. "Can you believe they were drinking on the job?" She laughed. "I know. You can believe it, can't you? People today." She shook her head the way Nana used to.

"Anyway," Mackenzie went on. "The client complained about the job the crew was doing and sure enough, they've made a mess of this man's house."

She smiled. "It's so pretty, Nana. It used to be a barn, only the owner, a contractor, turned it into a house. I know what you're thinking. People living in a cow barn, but it really is beautiful."

She sighed, thinking back over her lousy day. "So, I fired the crew, and it looks like I'm going to have to go in and do the painting myself." This was the first time Mackenzie had admitted to herself that this was the only way she would be able to get the job done. She would have to go herself to Ben Gordon's. "I'm going to advertise for some more help, but in the meantime, this job has to be done. The client has a business restoring houses. I think he could send some jobs my way if he's pleased with the work I do."

Mackenzie thought of Ben and a hard lump rose unexpectedly in her throat.

She considered telling her grandmother about him. About how she knew him. But she didn't want to worry her grandmother . . . just in case she could hear her.

She clapped her hands together, coming to her feet. "So that was the excitement for the day. Now how about if I get that Jell-O and we have some? Hmm?" She brushed her fingertips across her grandmother's cheek. She was a pretty woman, even at this age and in this state. "Then I have to go," Mackenzie said. "I know you like me to stay and watch *Jeopardy* reruns with you, but I have to go home and prepare for a meeting at the church tomorrow night. The Tree Festival is coming up quickly and I still need a few more sponsors. I'm hoping my committee can snag a few more for me."

Mackenzie walked away from the bed and headed for the refrigerator in the lounge. She felt like crying and didn't know why. It was hard coming to see Nana like this every day, but that wasn't it. She was used to it now. And yes, she'd had a lousy day at work, but that wasn't what made her teary either.

It was Bennett Gordon; he was upsetting her. It was Ben and regret that she hadn't accepted his offer for dinner. She was angry with herself, but whether it was for her refusal of his invitation, or for her regret, she didn't know.

Four

Ben thought he heard a sound in the driveway and rose from his chair at the kitchen table, coffee in hand. He glanced out the windows over the sink. The sound must have come from the road rather than his driveway.

"What are you so antsy about this morning?" Max grumbled, turning the page of the newspaper he had spread out on the table. He sprinkled sugar over his Corn Flakes.

Ben leaned on the counter and sipped his black coffee. "I'm not antsy. I just thought I heard someone in the driveway."

"You can go on about your business." Max slurped cereal off his spoon. "I can show the painters in. Be around most of the day if they need anything."

"I'm headed out, I just wanted to finish my coffee."

Father glanced at son skeptically.

Ben turned around to pour the rest of his coffee down the drain. Max knew him well, too well sometimes.

The truth was, he was purposefully waiting

around for the painters to arrive. He was stalling in the hope it was Mackenzie who showed up.

It was just a hunch, but he suspected she didn't have any other painting crews. There was something about the look on her face yesterday. After firing those bozos, she was bound to be short on painters. It would take time to hire a new, qualified crew. In the meantime, she needed to keep up her income so she could afford to make payroll when she did hire.

Ben knew from experience what it was like starting a business; he and his partners were right in the middle of it. He knew how important every job was at this stage of the game, and he knew how important income was. His guess was that Mackenzie Sayer would not let this opportunity to paint his house get away from her if she could help it. She was smart enough to know he could help her if he was satisfied with the job. She'd paint his living room herself if she had to.

Again, Ben heard the crunch of snow under tires. This time when he looked through the window he was rewarded with the sight of a Sayer and Sons van pulling into his drive. He waited long enough to see the driver in white coveralls and a green coat step out of the vehicle, then hurried out of the kitchen toward the mudroom.

Ben pulled open the door, offering his best smile. Zack swore it nearly made women swoon. " 'Morning."

Mackenzie glanced up, five-gallon buckets of paint in both hands. She did not look pleased to see him.

"Good morning," she said stiffly.

The smile didn't seem to work for her.

He held open the door and let her pass, intrigued that this woman seemed to be immune to many of the tricks he'd learned over the years.

"Anything else in the truck you need?" he asked.

"I can get it myself." He followed her into the living room. She wore her long, blond hair pulled back in a ponytail with a painter's cap covering the top of her head. She had turned the brim backward to protect her hair from any paint that might splatter. If she was wearing makeup, he couldn't tell. She was as fresh and beautiful as the first streaks of sunrise on a winter day, and as chilly as this morning's temperature.

"I'm on my way out, I don't mind."

She eyed him. "The roller with the long handle and the stepladder." She shrugged off her coat and laid it on a couch he'd covered with an old sheet.

Ben hurried out to the van, not bothering to throw on a coat. He was back in a minute with the ladder and her roller.

Max was leaning in the doorway, sipping his coffee, talking to Mackenzie. She smiled as she answered.

Ben wondered why his father deserved that big, beautiful smile and he didn't. But then Max always had had a way with females, females from babies to centenarians.

They were discussing the weather.

"They say it's warming up outside," Max observed, "but it didn't feel like it to me when I went out for the paper."

Mackenzie opened a paint can. "Snow's melted

some, so it must be. But you're right, certainly didn't feel it this morning."

As Ben leaned the ladder against the wall, he caught Max's eye. His dad, the sly dog, knew now what Ben had been antsy about. He knew why his son had lingered over breakfast.

"Well, back to my paper," Max said with a twinkle in his eyes. "You need anything, little lady, just give me a holler."

Ben stood awkwardly in the middle of his living room. He couldn't for the life of him figure out why he felt so weird in Mackenzie's presence. "Could I get you some coffee?" he asked. "Dad just made a fresh pot."

"He already offered." She flashed a perfunctory smile and went back to pouring the paint. "Thanks, but no thanks."

"Well, if you don't need anything—"

"Not a thing." She picked up the paint tray and walked to the far side of the room.

What was with this woman? Was she really this upset that he had complained about his windows being painted shut? Somehow, he didn't think so. Was it because he had asked her out on a date?

He took a step toward her. "Listen, Mackenzie, about yesterday."

She had dipped the short-handled roller into the paint and moved it up and down the wall with fine, smooth movements. She was obviously not going to cut him any breaks.

"I'm sorry if I offended you, asking you out the way I did." He waited.

There was a moment of silence between them,

but he could tell by the way her body movement had changed that she wanted to say something.

"It's all right," she said finally. "I wasn't offended, just . . . surprised."

He thought it was an odd thing to say. Why would she be surprised? Surely a woman as attractive as her was used to men asking her out. He wasn't sure how to respond. "I guess I came on a little fast. I really didn't mean to." He took a chance. "But the offer still goes. Just dinner, maybe a movie. We could talk about business in town. Maybe exchange some notes."

She finally turned to face him. She was a striking sight, so tall and willowy, all dressed in white. She could have been on the Aspen ski slopes had it not been for the paint roller in one hand. "Are you asking me to meet you to talk about business or are you asking me on a date?"

He wasn't used to women being so forthright. He generally saw women as coy, and not necessarily dishonest, but devious. Her candor unnerved him a little. "Well," he scratched behind his ear. Why *was* he asking her out? He didn't date. But he did like her. No, he didn't even know her well enough to say he liked her. It was just that she *intrigued* him. And if she was going to be forthright, he might as well be the same. "I guess I was hoping for a date date, but a business meeting would work, too."

That made her chuckle. "I'll think about it."

So, she did find him attractive. At least maybe just a little bit. His chest swelled with confidence. "You'll think about the business meeting or the date date?" he teased.

Her chuckle of amusement turned to laughter and the whole room echoed with the bright sound. "Aren't you employed?"

He was grinning now, feeling like himself again. "Sure. I've got a job."

"They why don't you go to it and let me get to mine?"

Ben left the house tossing his keys into the air and catching them, whistling as he went.

Mackenzie let out an audible sigh of relief when Ben walked out the door. She had expected to find him here waiting for her, or rather for her painters, but she was still nervous about talking to him. If there was any other way she could have this job without being here herself, she would have done it. Unfortunately, there was no alternative, so she would repaint Ben Gordon's living room and she would do a terrific job, not because she needed references from him, but because she always did a good job.

She was thankful Ben didn't comment about her arriving alone. She knew he knew that she didn't have a crew that was free. She knew he knew that she needed this job. He could have been a real jerk about it, but he hadn't been.

Max walked into the living room, watching her roll the roller up and down the wall. "You know, it wouldn't hurt, a date with my boy."

Mackenzie turned, a little embarrassed. "You were listening to our conversation?"

Max grinned. "A privilege that comes with old age."

He was as charming as his son. Perhaps this was where the Gordon male charm had begun.

Mackenzie went back to painting. "I don't date much."

"He doesn't date at all."

She chuckled. He was pulling her leg now. "Yeah, right, I'll believe that. An attractive, educated man in Land's End, who doesn't work in the chicken plant? I would imagine the single ladies are lining up outside his door to take him out."

Max grinned over the rim of his coffee mug. "Actually they're lining up to take me out."

She laughed, shaking her head.

"So are you?" Max questioned.

"Am I what?"

"Going to go out with my son."

"I told him I would think about it."

"He needs a good woman, you know. All men do." He slurped his coffee. "I keep telling him that, but he doesn't listen."

Mackenzie kept the roller steady, moving it up and down the wall with slow, precise movements. She liked to paint walls because it was a no-brainer once you managed the proper technique; she found it very soothing. "You said he doesn't date. Why not?"

Max exhaled, making his lips vibrate. "He and his partners—all friends since they were in grade school—made this agreement. Hell, it was months back when they were forming their corporation. It was supposed to be a joke. They swore to each other they wouldn't date anymore, said they'd had their share of women. Apparently my son was the only one fool enough to take the oath seriously."

Max walked over to the couch, ghosted with a sheet, and perched himself on the arm. "The other two regained their senses. A hurricane blew Owen's ex-wife in and they remarried not long ago. Zack met a lady doctor here in town, and we celebrated their nuptials just this last weekend."

Mackenzie wondered if Ben wanted all this information shared. Her guess was that he did not.

Sworn off women? So why had he asked her out? she wondered.

"Well." Max slapped his knee. "I guess I might as well get moving. I've got to run next door and fix the neighbor's garbage disposal and then I've got my exercise class at the pool at the senior center."

Mackenzie felt a pang of regret. Her grandmother had never taken an aquatic exercise class. She had kept to herself all the years Mackenzie was gone. The only time she went out was to church or to shop. Bingo in the church rectory had been her big outing once a month and never when the weather was bad. Now her grandmother never would swim in the senior center pool or talk again to a neighbor about a broken garbage disposal.

"You have a nice day," Max called as he went into the kitchen.

"You, too."

Mackenzie took a portable radio from her backpack and tuned in an oldies rock station. She sang away the morning as she painted, took a short break for lunch, and sang away the afternoon. She tried not to think about Ben or about what she would say when he asked her about going out again. She had a feeling he would definitely ask.

The shadows grew long on the walls as she began to seal the paint cans for the day. It was quickly growing dark outside and though she had turned on lamps in the room, artificial light wasn't good for a painter.

Mackenzie was just wrapping her roller in plastic wrap to take back to the office to wash in a utility sink when she heard someone come in the back door. It was Ben; she knew it before she saw him. She could tell by the way he walked, heavy-footed and sure of himself.

"Hey there," he said cheerfully. He was flipping through a stack of mail.

"Hi." She didn't know if she should smile or not. She didn't want him to think she was suddenly hot for him.

He looked up from the mail at the walls she had painted. "Looks nice. Better than nice, great."

"I'll bring my scaffolding with me tomorrow, start up high," she explained. What she had accomplished today wasn't any big deal, any decent painter could have done it, but his compliment still gave her a rush. She wondered what he would think of one of her paintings, if he saw it. Would he like the way she depicted the shades of a cornstalk or the feathering of a goose? Did he even like local landscapes or was he into modern art—pictures of things that didn't look like anything?

There were no pictures hung on the walls in the living room, of course. They had all been taken down by the paint crew.

"So, what do you think about tonight?"

She stood tall, stretching her lower back. She knew that by bedtime it would ache. She didn't do much painting because her days were filled with overseeing her employees, purchasing supplies, doing the bookkeeping and trying to scout out more business. "Tonight?"

"What? You're going to make me ask again?" He tossed the mail onto the couch, amused. "Because I will."

Mackenzie felt a sense of panic. What was she going to say?

"Mackenzie, would you like to go out with me?"

She dropped her radio into her backpack. "I . . . I have a meeting."

"After the meeting?"

She glanced at him, suddenly feeling clever. "You could go with me to the meeting. It's open to anyone. Lots of business men and women from town will be there." She slung her backpack over her back. "We could grab something to eat after that."

There. She'd said it. It was going to happen. Twenty years late, but she was going out with Ben Gordon.

"Can I pick you up?"

"Nope." She grabbed her paint roller. "Meet me at the Methodist church on Main. Seven."

Then she strode out of his house, feeling lighter on her size ten feet than she had in years.

Ben arrived five minutes early for Mackenzie's meeting in the basement of the local Methodist church. It wasn't until he was inside the door that it occurred to him that he hadn't asked her what the meeting was for. A group of men and women from town were milling around the classroom, getting coffee in Styrofoam cups and taking their seats. He knew quite a few of those in the room.

"Ben!" George Antle, the city planner, waylaid him just inside the door. The robust fiftysomething man thrust out his hand and pumped Ben's. "Good to see you here. Good to see you're really becoming a part of this community."

Becoming a part of the community? Ben thought. No, he was just coming by to pick up his date, right? Ben eyed Mackenzie at the front of the room. She was busy pulling papers from a knapsack and didn't see him.

"Good to see you, Ben." Alice Carpenter, the town librarian smiled.

Ben had dated her daughter, Laura, in high school. If he recalled correctly, Laura had none of the stereotypical traits one associated with a librarian. He'd had quite a good time with Miss Carpenter in the backseat of his dad's car.

"Nice to see you, Mrs. Carpenter." Ben stirred his coffee with one of those little sticks. "How's Laura?"

The librarian beamed. "Oh, she's wonderful. Mother of three. Her eldest, Joey, is taking first place at all his local swim meets in the butterfly." She brushed Ben's arm with her hand. "He may very well be an Olympic hopeful in another ten years."

Ben nodded and steered away from the librarian. He was hoping to speak with Mackenzie. Maybe he could just wait outside for her, but before he reached the head table, she spoke.

"If you will all take your seats," Mackenzie said

with such authority that Ben grabbed the closest chair, "we can get started."

"And the sooner we get started, the sooner we get out of here," said one of the men Ben didn't recognize.

Everyone laughed.

"Absolutely, Charlie." She lifted her gaze to address the entire group.

Ben couldn't help noticing how attractive she was. She had changed into blue jeans and a white oxford shirt. She wore loafers with heels that made her even taller than she was—another sign of her confidence in herself. He blond hair fell loose down her back like a shimmering sheet of spun gold. She wore a little lipstick, maybe color on her cheeks, but again, no obvious makeup. The woman was downright radiant.

"I'll take a report from each of the committee chairs in a sec," Mackenzie said, "but the reason we're really here is to see how many more tree sponsors we have. How's everyone been doing?"

Several people offered that they had found one or two more sponsors.

Ben gathered that they were discussing the annual Festival of Trees the city sponsored. Each year, businesses and individuals donated trees and ornaments. Everyone in town paid admission to see the "festival of lights" a week before Christmas and then the trees were auctioned off.

Mackenzie listened patiently, nodding. "Excellent. The numbers are looking better." She was tallying on a sheet of paper in front of her. "But we could still use some more sponsors. We've got to talk to our neighbors, to the shopkeepers we patronize. The more sponsors we have, the more trees we'll have and the more money we'll make for the adult community day-care center we're trying to get built."

George Antle, who sat behind Ben, gave him a poke in the shoulder. "How about you, Ben?"

"Me?" Ben glanced at Mackenzie. He could have sworn he saw her smile behind her clipboard.

"You. I didn't hear your name on the list. Didn't hear Land's End Renovations's name. You guys ought to sponsor a tree."

"I don't know," Ben stalled. The entire room had become quiet. Everyone was looking at him, including Mackenzie.

"What do you mean, you don't know?"

"Well, I don't know anything about sponsoring a tree—"

"Horse-hockey." George sat back in his seat. "Put Land's End Renovations down for a tree," he called jovially. "No, better yet, give them two. I hear through the grapevine that they're doing very well financially."

Several people chuckled.

Ben considered protesting. It wasn't that he was against supporting the Festival of Trees, he just wasn't certain this was the way he would have gone about it on his own. He met Mackenzie's gaze. She was waiting. If he was going say no, this was the time to do it.

Of course he wouldn't say no. He didn't mind supporting a good cause like this. His father was still in good health, both mentally and physically, but down the road, who knew? He might need this kind of support some day. And there were many people in the community who he knew could use it now. His partners wouldn't mind making this donation either. And after all, how difficult could this be? He'd hand over the money and the company's name would go on the tree and in the brochure.

She was still watching him and he knew by the look on her face that she knew he would make the donation.

Hoodwinked, Ben thought, not sure whether he was amused or annoyed. He'd been hoodwinked by an Amazon painter.

Five

"You set me up, didn't you?" Ben questioned the minute Mackenzie opened her car door. She had followed him to the Pizza Palace in her own vehicle. A date, but not quite a date.

She tried to conceal her smile as she grabbed her leather backpack off the passenger's seat and climbed out of her sports car, all legs and hair. "I did no such thing."

"I could just as easily have met you after your meeting." They walked side by side, across the street to the restaurant. It was so cold out that the warmth of their breath formed white clouds. An angel attached to a pole and framed in white lights glimmered overhead. An entire line of angels danced and twinkled down the old-fashioned Main Street. "There was no need for me to be there, except to be duped."

"It's for a good cause," she said innocently, flinging her bag over one shoulder.

Her leather jacket and black, wool scarf were very hip for Land's End. Zack and Owen were always giving Ben a hard time about his leather jacket.

"What are you griping about?" she asked. "I'm sure you and your business partners want to contribute to the community. It makes great PR. Everyone in town will know what swell guys you are."

"Everyone already knows what swell guys we are. And you could have just asked me if I wanted to sponsor a tree." He opened the door for her.

"Two trees." She winked, obviously pleased with herself and not feeling the least bit guilty. "We got you for two trees."

"Two," he corrected.

"So would you have sponsored a tree, two trees, if I'd asked?"

"Maybe."

He led her to his favorite table. The Pizza Palace was probably a dive compared to the kinds of places Mackenzie was used to, but the food was good and there weren't a lot of choices of places to eat in Land's End if you wanted to avoid fast food. Ben had been a fast-food junkie in his early years, but he was pushing forty fast and his middle just wouldn't tolerate that kind of fat and calories.

She started to take off her coat and he helped her. She tossed it on the vinyl bench seat along with her bag and slid in. "Maybe?" She lifted one lovely arched eyebrow.

"Maybe . . . or maybe not," he conceded sheepishly. He handed her a menu. "But that's not the point."

She flipped open her menu. She was unbelievably attractive when she was being sassy. He couldn't take his eyes off her, even to look at the menu.

"The point," she explained without looking up, "is that you got your date, and I have a sponsor for two more trees. More trees means more money for the community adult day care this town desperately needs." She paused. "Pasta or pizza?"

"Pardon?"

She glanced over the top of her menu. "Are we having pasta or pizza? I'm starved."

Her grin was infectious. He liked this woman, liked her a lot. She was definitely her own person and he admired that. She wasn't afraid to express herself, that was for sure. The women he had dated had always waited for him to take the lead with everything, from what they were going to order at a restaurant to when to use the bathroom. After a while, it became absurd. "I don't know what we're having. What do you feel like?"

She thought a minute. "Pizza and beer." She folded the menu and tossed it on the table. "You decide what kind. I'll eat anything."

He tucked the menus behind the napkin dispenser at the end of the table next to the wall. Maybe he'd spoken too soon. She wanted him to order. She'd regret that decision. "Pineapple and Canadian bacon."

Her eyes widened. "You're kidding, right?"

He laughed. "Pepperoni would be fine."

"No! I love pineapple and bacon pizza. No one else on earth will eat it but me."

The waitress came to the table and plucked a pencil from behind her ear. "Hey, Ben."

"Evening, Lucy." Lucy was only nineteen and had a three-year-old. She worked long hours to support herself and her little boy. She wasn't well educated, or particularly attractive, but she was a nice girl. "How are you this evening?"

"I'm good. I went over to the community college like you told me to and guess what?" She beamed.

"What?"

"I signed up for one of those classes. They say I can take the class and then take my GED. After that, I can get in real college classes."

"Told you you could do it."

Lucy blushed. "What can I get you for?"

"A pitcher of beer—light." He looked to Mackenzie for approval.

She nodded.

"And a large pineapple and Canadian bacon, deep dish."

"With extra cheese," Mackenzie added.

Lucy gave a nod and bopped off to put in the order.

"Extra cheese?" Ben questioned with amusement.

"What, you don't like extra cheese? Everyone likes extra cheese."

"I do. Love it. It's just that most of the women I've dated would have ordered the small salad with the fat-free dressing and a glass of water. I didn't realize women ate pizza and drank beer."

"Well, you've obviously been dating the wrong women. After a day of work, I'd like to eat the whole pizza myself and order two pitchers of beer."

He laughed. "Today was that bad?"

"No, not really. I just had a lot on my mind." She looked down at her hands, rubbing off a speck of dried paint. "Actually today was nice. I only checked in with the office a couple of times and everything was running smoothly. It was a pleasant change, working at your place. I like getting to

paint once in a while. It gives me time to think—
you know, refocus."

Lucy brought them a pitcher of beer and two
cold glass mugs. Ben poured.

Mackenzie lifted her mug. "Cheers."

He clinked his glass against hers. "Cheers."

Ben lifted the mug to his lips and heard his name
called. Out of the corner of his eye, he spotted
Savannah, his friend Zack's ten-year-old daughter.
She walked toward his table.

"Hi, Uncle Ben."

"Hey, sweetie." He motioned to Mackenzie.
"This is my friend Mackenzie. And this," he told
his date, "is my buddy Savannah."

"Nice to meet you," Savannah said politely, her
blond braids swinging. "Dad and Kayla ordered
pizza. I just got done with band practice, but we
have to get take out because I still have home-
work." She rolled her eyes.

"How was band practice?" Ben sipped his beer.

"Good, except Jacob Akers dropped gum into
Melissa Barker's tuba and he's getting kicked out
if his mom doesn't pay for the cleaning."

Ben nodded. He liked Savannah but he didn't
really know any other children. She was so strange
and so wonderful at the same time that sometimes
she seemed like a creature from some distant uni-
verse.

"Pizza's up, Savannah," Lucy called from the
counter.

The little girl flashed a bright smile. "See you
later, Uncle Ben. Nice to meet you, Mackenzie. I
hope I'll see you again," she said meaningfully.

Ben groaned as the girl bounced off.

Mackenzie laughed. "What was that supposed to mean?"

"I think my nosy little buddy is trying to say that she approves of my date. Usually I come here with the guys or a copy of the daily paper."

Mackenzie nodded, sipping her beer. "Your dad told me you don't date much."

"You and my father discussed my dating habits?"

"And his."

He groaned again. "Great."

"So why don't you?"

"What?" He poured more beer for both of them.

"Date."

"Aren't we supposed to be talking about the weather or how good the beer is?" he asked, leaning forward to get closer to her. "That's usually how my first dates go."

"Do you like talking about the weather?"

"Not particularly."

"Good." She licked the beer foam from her upper lip. "Because I don't either. So why don't you date?"

"No pussyfooting around with you, is there?"

She looked him right in the eye. "Nope. Too old, too jaded."

Ben lowered his voice an octave, leaning forward again. Suddenly the public place seemed private. "I'm sorry to hear that—the jaded part."

Mackenzie leaned back on the bench, crossing her arms almost protectively over herself. "I'm also old enough to know all the lines, so don't try to tell me you wish you'd been there to 'protect me.'"

Ben could almost hear the sizzle in her tone. He sat back. He had been thinking just that, but his motives had been entirely sincere. He did feel a strange sense of protectiveness toward her and he had no idea why. He made a mental note of that for the future. If he could wrangle a future date, he'd be more careful about saying things like that. Most women liked to hear those kinds of niceties. Obviously, she was not most women.

Lucy arrived with the pizza, rescuing Ben from the awkward moment. He put two slices on Mackenzie's plate and served them to her.

He grabbed two slices for himself. "To answer your question, I stopped dating because after a while it didn't seem healthy for me." He glanced up. "I know, it's very new millennium for a man to be concerned about his mental health." He shook his head. "I just seemed to be spinning my wheels. Dating too many women. The wrong women."

"Met most of them in bars? Bars or castoffs from someone else?"

He nodded. Hearing a woman say it out loud made him feel like a schmuck. But it wasn't as if he had forced himself upon any of those women. Mostly, they came to him. In fact, all of them came to him, except this one.

"Been there," she said quietly, taking a bite of pizza. "Done that."

"You, too?"

"Looking for love in all the wrong places," she sang.

He laughed. "So how did you solve the problem?"

"Same as you."

Again, their gazes met and Ben knew it sounded

ridiculous, but he felt as if he had made a connection with her.

"I gave up dating for the Saturday night movie of the week, charity work, and microwave popcorn." She picked a piece of pineapple from her pizza and popped it into her mouth.

"I guess I should feel honored that you agreed to go out with me," he said, feeling just that.

"Guess you should." But then she smiled and he knew she was teasing him.

"I'm glad you did, even if it will cost a bundle in Christmas tree ornaments." He took a chance and slid his hand across the table to cover hers. "I mean that."

She held his gaze, her green eyes dark and unreadable. She made no move to hold his hand, but she didn't pull away, either. "I almost think you do, Bennett."

They studied each other for a long moment, as if playing a game of chicken. He was the one who finally pulled his hand away. He reached for another piece of pizza. "You know, when I walk you to the car, I'm going to want to kiss you." His tone was light, but he meant it.

"You know, I'm not going to let you," she answered, just as carefree.

"I guess that means going home with me is out of the question." He was enjoying the banter . . . the chase per se. "More pizza?"

"Absolutely on both counts."

She flashed a grin comparable to his own, and just that suddenly Ben was afraid he was in love.

* * *

The phone was ringing when Ben walked into the house. He glanced upward in the dark living room to see light spilling from his father's bedroom down the hall. Max was home.

The phone rang again. In a minute, the answering machine would pick up.

Apparently, Max wasn't going to.

Ben fumbled under a dust cloth and picked up the phone. "Hello."

"Zhere has been a sighting," came a voice over the phone. It was Zack and he was speaking in a fake German accent. "Ze sighting has not yet been confirmed, but reliable sources say it is true."

"Zack?" Ben frowned. "Have you gone off your medication? You know what the doctor said," Ben teased. "If you can't take your medicine regularly, he's going to lock you up in the funny farm again."

"It is true, then?" Zack questioned, still using the goofy accent.

Ben had a feeling he knew what Zack was calling about, but he wasn't going to play along. "What's true?"

"Ze girl."

Ben shrugged off his coat. "I had pizza with a friend."

"Savannah said she was a looker." Zack dropped the accent.

"Yeah, she's pretty."

"What's her name?"

"Mackenzie, Mackenzie Sayer."

"You're dating the guy who screwed up your paint job?"

Ben carried the cordless phone into the kitchen and switched on an overhead light. "He's not a guy;

he's a woman. I mean she's a woman." Just talking about Mackenzie made him feel weird—lightheaded. He had really enjoyed his evening with her. Maybe a little too much for comfort.

Ben pulled open the refrigerator door. "And I'm not dating her. We went out for pizza."

"Ah-ha, I see."

Ben grabbed the pitcher of orange juice and closed the door behind him. He didn't like Zack's tone; he knew that tone. It had the same resonance he had used with Zack only a few short months ago when Zack had started dating the lady doctor who was now his wife. "You don't see. There's nothing *to* see."

"She nice?"

"Yeah, she's nice." He took a glass from the cupboard and poured himself some juice. "But she doesn't like me."

"She went out for pizza with you, but she doesn't like you?" Zack's voice grew a little distant as he shouted to someone else in his house. "He went out with a beautiful woman who doesn't like him!"

Ben heard Kayla's laughter in the background. "Well, she kind of likes me. She just doesn't know it yet."

"Mm-hmm," Zack intoned. "And she went out with you why?"

"To get me to buy trees."

"She's also a tree farmer?"

Ben drained the glass. "No. It's one of those decorated trees for the Festival of Trees they have here every year. You know, a benefit kind of thing. This year the money is going toward setting up a day-care program for elderly people."

Just then Max walked into the kitchen. "You're going to put me in day care? My memory's a little shy at times, but I don't think I'm ready for day care."

"I'm not putting you in day care," Ben said.

"That's a good thing," Zack said. "Though I might enjoy it once or twice a week."

Ben groaned. He felt as if he were in a fun house and couldn't get out. "I'm talking to Dad, not you. No one's going to adult day care. Unless maybe it's me to get away from you all!"

Max waved as if Ben were talking nonsense. He poured himself a glass of juice and shuffled out of the kitchen in his slippers.

"So you're sponsoring a tree?" Zack picked up where the conversation had left off without skipping a beat. "Very noble of you, buddy."

"Actually you're sponsoring one, too."

"What? I didn't have a date with the leggy blonde."

"Not you personally, the business. Land's End Renovations is sponsoring two Christmas trees."

"And you're going to decorate these things?" Zack questioned with a laugh.

"Sure. I mean, I guess so." Ben leaned over the sink to rinse out his glass. "I don't know. I'll buy a box of glass balls and throw them up on the thing."

Zack started laughing.

"What? What's so funny?"

"You have to have a theme, buster."

Ben frowned. "A theme?"

"You've been to these things before," Zack said. "You can't just throw glass balls up on a tree. People are going to pay good money to buy decorated trees. Each tree has a theme, you know, 'teddy bears,' 'red birds,' 'hearts and lace.' Horse-hockey like that."

"You're kidding me."

Zack sniggered. "You must really like this woman to get snookered into something like this."

"Gotta go, Zack. I have to kill a lady painter."

"Later, dude," Zack laughed.

Ben had no sooner hung up when the phone rang again. "I'm not talking to you anymore, Zack. Go to bed."

"This is Owen. Why aren't you talking to Zack? He give you a hard time about your date?"

Ben pushed the orange juice pitcher back into the refrigerator. "You know, too? What, you have surveillance equipment set up at the Pizza Palace?"

"Better than that. A network of teenyboppers. Savannah called us."

Ben didn't know why he felt so defensive. Maybe because he'd been so adamant about not dating, even when the other two fell from grace. "Look, it was pizza and beer."

"Just wanted to confirm." There was amusement in Owen's voice. "Abby says to tell you to bring your date over Saturday night for poker."

"We'll see," Ben grumbled.

"He'd love to!" Owen hollered to his wife.

"I'm hanging up now," Ben said. "See you tomorrow."

Ben hung up the phone and pulled the phone book from the drawer. He looked up Sayer, but there was no listing for Mackenzie. Next, he called operator assistance. Bingo!

Ben perched on the edge of the kitchen counter and punched her number. She picked up on the second ring. He didn't give her a chance to say anything more than hello.

"A theme? My trees have to have a theme?"

Six

"May I ask who's calling, please?" Mackenzie dripped with honey. It was Ben, of course. She'd been hoping and waiting and trying not to do either, since she got home from the Pizza Palace. She was so glad he called. She hadn't even given him her phone number.

"You know who this is. It's Ben." He was trying to sound perturbed, but she could hear the amusement in his voice. He liked quick wit, just as she did.

"Bennett Gordon?" she questioned. "That Ben?"

"You didn't tell me I had to actually decorate the damned trees using a theme."

Mackenzie curled up on the couch and pulled an afghan her grandmother had crocheted for her onto her lap. The multicolored throw had been with her through college, various apartments, and numerous towns. It was like an old, comfy friend.

"Of course you have to decorate the trees. Why would people buy Christmas trees at the auction if they weren't decorated in an interesting way?"

"The natural look?" he asked hopefully. "Bare? Or maybe a few cheap glass balls?"

"Sure, you can go for the natural look. That's

popular around here. Cinnamon cut ornaments, dried fruit, raffia garland. Great idea."

"That's not what I mean."

"Well, you have plenty of time to get your thoughts together," she told him, turning off the TV with the remote. She'd been watching an old Humphrey Bogart movie. She loved Humphrey Bogart. With the TV dark, there was no light in the living room except for what came from the kitchen. It was kind of neat, sitting in the dark, under the afghan, talking to Ben. Intimate, in an exhilarating way. "I need to know your themes by Wednesday and the trees have to be done by the following Wednesday."

"That's less than two weeks!"

"Well, it wouldn't do much good to sell the trees after Christmas, now would it, Bennett?"

He chuckled, his voice low and sexy. "I love it when you call me Bennett."

Mackenzie felt her cheeks grow warm. She didn't know where this was going with Ben. She didn't know where she wanted it to go. She'd given up the idea of finding a mate long ago. She had convinced herself she wasn't suited to be half of a partnership, but Ben made her wish she were.

Then there was the little matter of who she was; she knew she needed to tell him. If she was going to hold all of that high school nonsense against him, he at least ought to know it. She just couldn't figure out a way to approach the subject. And somewhere deep inside she knew she was afraid to tell him. He liked Mackenzie Sayer; she could hear it in his voice. She had seen it in his eyes. Would he feel the same way when he discovered that she was Margaret Mackenzie Sayer?

"I'll be there in the morning to start painting again. You want to leave me a key?"

"I can wait around."

"You don't have to." She wanted him to wait around, of course. She ran her fingers over her bare feet. Her toenails needed painting. "I know you have to get to work."

"I don't mind," he said smoothly. "In fact, you come a little early and I'll make you breakfast."

She felt a little trill of excitement. Ben Gordon was pursing her. "Would that be another date?"

His voice was warm in her ear. "Only if you want it to be."

"Actually, it's you I'm concerned about. Your dad said you don't date. That would be two dates in the same week for a man who doesn't date."

He laughed. "So it's not a date. It's breakfast. What time can I expect you?"

"I go to the gym at six thirty. Eight okay?"

"Perfect. Hotcakes, or eggs and bacon?"

"Yes."

Again, he laughed. "I like a woman who knows how to eat. See you in the morning, Mackenzie."

" 'Night," she murmured.

When she hung up, she sat on the couch in the dark for a moment, the phone cradled in her hand. She really liked Ben. The question was, did she like him for who he was now or was she still pining for the Ben she had known in high school?

Mackenzie heard a whine and glanced up to see her grandmother's old dog, Howard, come out of her bedroom. She knew he had been on her bed again; he had that guilty look on his face.

"Hey, boy, how's my Howie?" she crooned.

The dog wagged his graying tail frantically and pushed his head beneath her hand to be petted.

Mackenzie stroked the dog's short coat, scratching him behind the ears. When she'd returned to Land's End after her grandmother had the stroke, she'd been forced to sell Grandmother's house to pay for the nursing home. Selling the house and putting Nana in Westview had left Howard homeless. At the time she tried to convince herself that it would be better for Howie if she put him up for adoption. She didn't have time with the new business and with Nana so ill to care properly for an aging dog. Luckily guilt had set in and when she moved to the apartment, she'd brought Howie with her.

The dog whined and put his front paws up on the couch. Mackenzie rubbed his back.

Howard was a mutt. Old and ugly. He looked to be a cross between a yellow lab and a German shepherd, but there was no way to know. Nana had found him as a pup, eating garbage out of a dumpster behind a fast-food place. She had taken Howie home nine years ago and he had been her companion ever since. It was Howie who had alerted a neighbor when Nana had her stroke. If it hadn't been for the dog's manic barking out the window, Nana might have died alone in the house with no one but her dog to know.

Now that Mackenzie and Howie had settled into a routine, she was grateful he had given her the sad-doggie look when she'd tried to tell him he was going to the animal shelter. His pitiful whine had made her wonder if he actually understood what she was saying. Howie had licked her hand and begged Mackenzie to keep him. Mackenzie, who liked her house neat and tidy, who did not like puffs of dog hair under the kitchen table, now slept with the mutt. He was there to see her off in the morning when she went to work and was waiting at the door when she returned at night. Howie was her best friend in the world.

"Okay, boy," Mackenzie said, trying to rise from the couch. "Time for bed is it?"

The dog wagged his tail and started for the bedroom, glancing over his shoulder to be sure she was following him.

Mackenzie wondered what Ben Gordon would think if he knew she slept with a dog. He'd probably be jealous. She clicked the kitchen light off with a smile.

"So tell me exactly what I have to do with these trees." Ben carried a plate of steaming pancakes to the kitchen table.

Mackenzie brought the bowl of scrambled eggs and the plate of bacon over and they both sat down.

Ben picked up the plate of pancakes and held them out to her. "You know I'm still thinking about that kiss I didn't get last night," he said, smiling. "You think you'd be willing to trade this plate of steaming hotcakes for a measly peck?"

Charming. Entirely too charming.

"Do you think you'd be willing to trade your arm

for those pancakes." She lifted her fork like a dagger. "Because if you don't hand them over—"

"I get the picture." He passed her the pancakes and she helped herself.

"Sponsoring a tree is simple," she said, letting the kiss conversation drop, though just the thought made her toes in her steel-toed work boots tingle. She hadn't kissed a man in months, not since she left Newark and her professor who claimed to be her boyfriend, though he'd only seen her once a week. "Decide what will go on the tree to express the theme you choose. Buy or make the ornaments, and decorate your designated tree, which will be set up at the church hall beginning next week."

Ben placed three pancakes on his plate and reached for the scrambled eggs. "Simple. Right. I don't know anything about decorating Christmas trees. I don't know what theme to pick."

"Be creative." She poured syrup over her pancakes. This was fun, having breakfast in this sunny room with Ben. She'd been eating breakfast alone for too long.

"I'm not creative. Not in that way, at least." His blue eyes twinkled with a hint of sexual innuendo, but it was light enough to be tantalizing rather than egotistical.

"Okay," Mackenzie tried a different tact, "what do you like?"

"What do I like?" He forked pancake into his mouth. "I like pancakes."

She gave him a stern look. "I'm not sure pancakes would work on a Christmas tree."

He knitted his brows. "And tools, I like tools. I know it's boorish, but I like power tools."

She sipped her orange juice. He had actually squeezed oranges for her this morning. Would she be considered a loose woman if she gave him that kiss he wanted in exchange for more freshly squeezed orange juice?

"Power tools would be interesting, but . . . a little heavy for blue spruce branches."

He threw up his hands. "I told you I'm not creative. I can't do this."

"You can. It will just take a little thought." She bit into a forkful of fluffy scrambled egg. Delicious. A man who could cook and was nice to look at first thing in the morning—how could she not want to kiss him?

"You could do it for me," Ben said slyly. He got up to pour them both more coffee.

"Oh, no." She laughed. "You're on your own here, buster. I have my own tree."

He poured the coffee from over her left shoulder. He smelled alluringly of shaving cream, shampoo, and maleness. "How are you decorating your tree?"

"Not telling."

"What do you mean, you're not telling?" He returned the pot to the coffeemaker and sat down across from her again. He was dressed casually in well-worn khakis and a cotton sweater that fit his athletic build quite nicely.

"It's supposed to be a surprise," she insisted. "That's part of the fun of the whole thing."

"I don't feel like I'm having fun."

"Oh, you will. Just give it a chance." She gestured with her fork. "Look at this as a challenge. You're a manly man. Manly men like challenges."

Finished with his plate, he rose, taking it to the sink. "Manly man? That doesn't sound complimentary."

"It wasn't meant to be a criticism." Stuffed, she pushed her plate away. "I just meant that men really enjoy challenges and if you see this project as a challenge, you might be better able to focus on it."

Raising a dark eyebrow, he swept away her plate. "Sounds like a lot of mumbo jumbo to me."

She followed him from the table, taking her empty juice glass with her. "This juice is great. Have any more?" She met him at the counter. He had that charming look on his face again, as if he were going to put the move on her. She resisted out of principle. "Don't tell me you want a kiss for the juice because I'll clobber you with this glass."

He lifted the pitcher from the counter and poured the last of the juice into her glass. "What would make you even suggest such a thing?"

She leaned against the counter, enjoying the juice and the flirtatious banter. This was part of the problem with dating these days. No one flirted. You met someone, shared a few drinks, and then went home with them. Now Ben was different; he knew how to flirt. Maybe as well as Bogart.

She sipped her juice. She wanted to kiss him. She liked the idea of sharing a first kiss here in the sunny kitchen early in the morning. But she wanted the kiss on her terms, not his.

Mackenzie reached around Ben and set her glass in the sink. He was rinsing off the dishes and putting them in the dishwasher.

"Well, thanks for breakfast. I guess I'd better get

to work." On impulse, she pressed a kiss to his cheek. A kiss, but not a real kiss.

Ben turned his head, a dirty plate still in his hand. His eyes were bright and warm. As he leaned forward to meet her lips, she pulled back a little.

"Let's not get greedy," she whispered playfully.

He nodded ever so slightly. Then he surprised her with a gentle, "Thanks."

The man was thanking her for a peck on the cheek! She grinned and walked away. "You're welcome."

Ben whistled to himself as he went down the hall to his office. He could hear the radio station Mackenzie was listening to downstairs in the living room as she painted. Breakfast had been nice, very nice. And she'd surprised him with her kiss. It seemed silly when he thought about it, but he liked the way she hadn't given right into him. Shoot, he'd had two dates with the woman and one innocent peck on the cheek was all he had gotten for his "troubles." The women he'd dated in the past were in his bed before he knew their full names.

Mackenzie was definitely a different breed of woman from the ones he had dated previously, and he definitely liked her. Neither his good looks nor the charm he knew he possessed swayed her. Part of it came naturally—from his dad, no doubt—but some of it was acquired charm.

He liked Mackenzie? Hell, he was crazy about her. It didn't make any sense to Ben. It was completely unlike him to fall for a woman. It was as if a part of him had gone crazy. But he couldn't stop thinking about her. Couldn't get enough of her. He'd never really pursued a woman before; he'd never had to. But this woman—he had to have her.

Ben sat at his desk and glanced over his calendar for the day. He had a couple of appointments but he had some phone calls to make. It was a busy schedule, but he was hoping he could get everything done and get back by the time Mackenzie was ready to knock off work. Maybe she'd want to go out to get something to eat.

He thought about her kiss and unconsciously touched his cheek. He could almost still feel her warm mouth on his skin. He wondered what it would be like to feel her lips on his. He wondered how long it would take him to find out.

Ben picked up the phone. He had one phone call to make before he made those business calls.

Owen picked up. "Hello."

" 'Morning," Ben said. They didn't have to identify themselves on the phone with each other. They'd been friends since they were ten and inherently recognized each other's voices. "May I speak to your bride?"

"My bride?"

"I want to talk to Abby, Owen. Is she around?"

"Are you around?" Owen said, obviously to Abby who was in the same room.

Ben glanced at the clock on his desk. It was eight forty-five. "Are you guys still in bed?" he asked. "I didn't mean to wake you."

"Yes, we're still in bed," Owen said. "But you didn't wake us."

Ben laughed. "Spare me the torrid details. Is she available or not?" He heard the phone being passed.

" 'Morning, Ben."

"Hey, I've got a favor to ask you."

"Yeah?"

"We . . . the company is sponsoring some Christmas trees for the festival in two weeks—"

"No way."

"No way what? I didn't even finish asking."

"You want to know if I'll decorate one of your trees for you, and the answer is no way."

Ben groaned. "Oh, come on, Abby. Be a buddy, be a pal."

"You made the commitment. Decorate the tree yourself."

"I can't decorate a tree. Men don't decorate trees. They dress up like lumberjacks and go out and fell trees, but they don't decorate them."

Abby was laughing. "The answer is no, Ben. I love you dearly, but I'm not letting you off this easily."

"What do you mean?"

"You donated those trees to get in good with the leggy painter. Owen told me all about it."

"Owen has a big mouth. Let me talk to the creep."

"Have a nice day," Abby said sweetly.

Owen got back on the phone. "That woman of yours is cold," Ben said. "Cold and unsympathetic."

"She just likes to see you squirm. As a matter of fact, we all do."

"See you at ten," Ben grumbled.

Ben could hear Owen grinning, even across the phone lines. "See you at ten."

Ben finished his phone calls and went back to the kitchen for another cup of coffee before he got on the road. His father was seated at the table eating cereal and reading the paper.

"You want me to make you some eggs or some pancakes, Dad? I already ate."

"Saw two plates in the dishwasher."

"Guilty as charged."

"She spend the night?"

Ben poured his coffee into a travel mug. His immediate impulse was to defend her; she wasn't that kind of woman. His need to protect her felt strange . . . but good in weird kind of way. "No, she didn't spend the night."

Max shoveled multigrain flakes into his mouth. "Good. I don't want to see you mess this up."

Ben rolled his eyes. A part of him wanted to tell his father about these unexpected feelings for Mackenzie, but he kept quiet. How could he explain it to Max if he didn't understand it himself? "Dad, there's no *this.*" At least not yet, there wasn't. "She was coming over to paint so we had breakfast together."

"You just keep telling yourself that." Max winked. "Make it go down smoother."

Ben wasn't ready to talk about Mackenzie with his father so he changed the subject. "You going to be home for dinner, Pop?"

"Nope. Taking the turtle out to the Chinese buffet. It's senior night. Ten percent off."

Ben chuckled. "Does she mind you calling her Myrtle the Turtle?"

"Hell, no, she doesn't mind. A good-looking man

like me, still got all my teeth. We're few and far between at this age."

"Well, if I don't see you, have a good time. Call me if you need a ride home."

"I can get my own ride home," Max grumbled, turning back to the paper.

"You can't take your date on the lawn tractor." When Max and Ben had agreed last spring that it was no longer a good idea for him to drive, Max had taken to tooling around town on their lawn tractor. At first, it had irritated Ben; it made him feel as if he wasn't taking proper care of his father. He could certainly transport him where he needed to go, or at least call the senior-center shuttle. It had taken months for Ben to realize that the lawn tractor was about independence. Once he understood where his father was coming from, he didn't mind so much.

"I'm not taking Myrtle on the lawn tractor." Max gave a contrary wave. "Go on with you. Leave me to read my paper in peace."

"All right." Ben walked by and brushed his father's shoulder with his hand. They weren't much for physical demonstrations of their love for each other, but that didn't make the love any less strong. "Have a good day, and, Pop?" Ben halted in the doorway.

Max glanced up. "Yeah?"

Ben lowered his voice. "Stay away from my painter."

Father and son made eye contact. Both were laughing as Ben headed out the door.

Seven

"Thanks, but I can't." Mackenzie tapped a paint can lid with a rubber mallet. It was five o'clock—quitting time.

Ben hovered close. "Just a quick bite. I won't keep you long."

"I can't, Ben. I really can't." She carried the paint can to the drop cloth along the wall. "I've got to go to the grocery store, stop to see someone, do laundry and—" She cut herself off. Why was she giving explanations? She had a right to say no to his invitation. She had a right to be hesitant to take this relationship any further.

She'd been thinking about Ben all day. He was a playboy. No matter what he or his father said about him changing his ways, it didn't change who Bennett Gordon was inside. He wasn't the type of man who could form a lasting relationship with a woman. He'd practically come right out and said it himself.

Mackenzie wrapped the paintbrush and roller in plastic, feeling weary. The unfortunate truth was that Ben wasn't going to give her anything permanent, and she wasn't going to settle for anything less. Not with this man, not with any. She was past that point in her life. Maybe that was the ultimate truth she'd accepted today. She'd realized that if she never found a man to love, she was okay with that. She had her business, her church, her charity work, her art and Nana. She could be content because for the first time in her life, she was content with who she was.

"Come on," Ben wheedled, as charming and appealing as ever. "It can be something quick—a salad at a fast-food place. Chinese takeout."

"No, thank you," she answered firmly.

When he didn't say anything else, she glanced at him. He looked like a whipped puppy, so forlorn that she almost gave in. Then she reminded herself that it was probably all an act. Ben was used to getting his way with women.

"I have to go," she said, grabbing her brush and roller and backpack. "I'll be back Monday morning."

He followed her to the back door. "Breakfast again?" There it was again, the charm that made a girl weak in the knees and consequently the brain as well.

"I don't think so." She waved over her shoulder as she stepped out into the darkness. " 'Night."

She heard the door close.

He didn't follow.

It was just as well. There was no sense in his asking anymore because she wasn't going out with him. She didn't want him to follow her.

Yes, she did.

A pathetic life she led, but it was hers.

Mackenzie climbed into the utility van, started up the engine and turned to look through the rear panel windows to back out of the driveway.

Just as she hit the gas, she heard a tap on the driver's side glass. She jerked around.

It was him.

Ben motioned for her to put down her window. He was standing in the snow, no coat, no shoes. Just stockinged feet.

"Was it something I said?" he asked.

"No." She shook her head.

"You're sure?"

She wasn't certain how to respond. What could she say? Yes, you did something wrong twenty years ago and I'm so immature that I can't forget it? Or yes, you did something wrong by being you. I'm attracted to you; I like you, but I don't want to?

If it didn't make sense in Mackenzie's head, she knew it wouldn't make any sense coming out of her mouth.

She exhaled, collecting her thoughts. "Ben, I'm tired and I really have to go."

"But I'll see you Monday?"

She nodded.

"Can I call you tonight?"

She hesitated, then nodded again. "I'll be home after *Wheel of Fortune.*" She liked to sit and watch the show with her grandmother; it had been one of her favorites.

He knitted his brows but didn't comment. "I'll call around eight, eight-thirty?"

She nodded, rolled up the window, and turned to back out again. She didn't look in the direction of the house until she was on the road beside his house. He stood on his front step, in his socks, waving. Smiling.

"Mackenzie, you're crazy," she said aloud as she

shifted the van into first and pulled away. "Why not take what he offers? A little companionship, maybe a little hanky-panky?"

Because she wanted more.

The phone rang at five after eight. Mackenzie had just changed into old sweatpants and a sweatshirt. She and Howard were sharing an omelet she'd whipped up after she arrived home from visiting Nana. The visit had been depressing; Nana seemed worse. She wasn't eating well and there had been discussion of inserting a feeding tube again. Mackenzie didn't know what to do, and she wished for the millionth time that she had someone to help her make the decision.

When the phone rang a third time, Howard looked up from the egg on his plate as if to say, "Well, are you going to answer it or not?"

Mackenzie scooped up the phone. "Hello."

"Hi. It's Ben."

"I know who it is." She smiled. "So what are you up to tonight?"

"Not much. Dad's out on a date. I had something to eat. I might read. I might watch a little TV."

"*A Christmas Carol* is on tonight. The old version."

"I didn't know that was on tonight," he said excitedly. "It's one of my favorites."

"Mine too. I like the remake with George C. Scott too, but this one's my favorite." She nibbled a bit of egg off her fork.

"What time is it on?"

"Nine. You going to watch it?"

She could hear clinking sounds in the background. He had to be emptying the dishwasher. "You bet." He paused, then his voice was quieter. "Hey, we could stay on the line and watch it together."

She laughed at the thought but was touched at the same time. Without thinking, she said, "Or you could come over and we could watch it together."

"You serious? Is that an invitation?"

Mackenzie hesitated, wondering if she was making a mistake, asking Ben over to her apartment. She had already turned down his offer for dinner. She wasn't generally a wishy-washy kind of person. She usually made a decision and stuck with it, but suddenly she realized she didn't want to be alone tonight. She was tired of the lonely nights. "That's a genuine invitation. Come on over. I'll make popcorn."

"I'll bring the Diet Pepsi."

She gave him her address. "When can I expect you?"

"In the time it takes me to ditch the slippers, find my coat, and get over there."

She laughed. "Wear the slippers if you like. We're pretty casual around here."

"We?"

"Howie and me."

His tone changed. "Howie?"

She knew what he was thinking. Who was Howie? Father? Worse, a son? Should she tell him Howie was a dog?

Nah. He was sounding a little too sure of himself; she'd let him squirm a little. "See you soon," she said and hung up.

* * *

By the time Ben rang the doorbell to her apartment, Mackenzie was ready for him. Ready and semicalm. She had made the decision not to change out of her sweatpants and sweatshirt; this was part of who she was. But she did run a comb through her hair and brush her teeth.

Howie barked wildly when the doorbell rang, and Mackenzie peered through the security peephole. Ben was standing at her door with a grocery sack in his arms. She, of all people, knew one couldn't judge a person by their looks, but she had to admit, he was looking damned good tonight in a rumpled, lazy kind of way.

"Hi." She felt oddly shy as she let him in. To her surprise, under his coat, he was wearing sweatpants, a sweatshirt . . . and slippers.

"Nice slippers," she commented, amused. Not many men would wear slippers in public, no matter how good a joke it was.

He wiggled his toes inside the old corduroy house shoes. "Glad you like them. You said casual." He held out his arm. "This is casual."

She showed off her ancient college sweatshirt and discount-store sweatpants. "This is casual here, too." Laughing, she closed the door behind him.

Howie barked and danced sideways, leaping in the air as he tried to catch Ben's attention.

"Howie, sit, boy," Mackenzie reprimanded. "We don't get many visitors," she explained. "He's very excited."

Ben raised an eyebrow as he reached down with his free hand to pet the dog. "This is Howie?"

She nodded. "My best buddy in the whole world."

Ben looked relieved. *"This* is Howie," he repeated.

"Yup. Howie's a dog." She took the grocery bag from him and carried it into the kitchen.

Ben followed. Howie followed him.

"You know, all the way over here I prepared myself for a two-year-old."

"A two-year-old?"

"When you said you and Howie would be waiting, I figured you meant you had a son. I mean, you could have. It's not as if I'd asked you if anyone lived with you."

"Would that have been a problem?" She took a two-liter bottle of soda out of the bag. There was red licorice, too. She loved red licorice.

He took off his coat. "Actually . . . no. On the ride over, I decided it wouldn't have been."

She grabbed two glasses and pushed them into his hand. "Ice." She went to the cupboard and located a bag of microwave popcorn. "Well, there's no one here but me and my dog. No offspring."

At the freezer door, he dropped ice cubes into the glasses. "Me neither."

She rolled her eyes. "Well, I assumed that, Mr. Playboy."

He knitted his brows. "You know, I can't put a finger on you, Mackenzie Sayer." He shook his head. "I'm usually on target about people, but I can't quite figure you out."

She met his gaze. She used to be bothered by her height, but over the years, she had discovered that there were advantages to being as tall as a man.

She liked being able to look directly into Ben's eyes. "What do you mean?" She shrugged, placing the popcorn bag into the microwave on the counter and pushing the right buttons.

The kitchen in the old apartment was sparse, but bright. Mackenzie had painted the entire place before she moved in to erase some of its dreariness and make it her own. The kitchen was a buttercup yellow, with a daisy print valance on the small window over the sink.

Mackenzie leaned against the counter, crossing her arms over her chest. She watched Ben. "What can't you figure out about me?"

"Well, you seem very confident of yourself, certainly self-assured when it comes to business, but you don't always seem to feel comfortable with your appearance." His tone was thoughtful.

She studied his face, not certain what to say.

"I don't know why. I mean, Mackenzie, you're drop-dead gorgeous. Most women would kill to have half the looks and the presence you have."

She gave a little laugh. "It's not all it's cracked up to be."

He nodded. "I would guess it isn't."

The microwave beeped and she turned her back to him. "And I didn't always look like this. There was a point in my life," she said hesitantly, "when I was heavy." She thought this might be the perfect opportunity to continue, to tell Ben who she was. But when she turned, he was standing right behind her, too close for comfort.

He smiled, his face gentle. He reached out and slowly pushed a lock of hair from the corner of her eye. "So you still see yourself as the fat girl inside?" he asked, seeming to understand.

She couldn't make herself look away. Here she was, holding a bag of popcorn in her hand, drowning in the gaze of the man of her dreams.

He was going to kiss her.

Mackenzie felt a flutter of panic in her chest, but she wanted him to kiss her. She wanted to feel his mouth on hers. She wanted to taste him.

Sure enough, Ben leaned closer. He took his time, giving her the opportunity to turn away.

She had no intention of saying no this time.

His mouth touched hers, warm and hesitant.

She closed her eyes wanting to savor the moment. She remembered once practicing kissing by pressing her lips to the bathroom mirror in her grandmother's house. She remembered pretending the mirror was Ben.

His lips were much warmer.

She let out a little sigh as he wrapped his arms around her waist and brushed her lips with the tip of his tongue. She eased her arms around his neck, still holding the bag of popcorn.

The kiss deepened, but Ben wasn't pushy. He didn't seem to feel the need to dominate that so many men demonstrated.

A trill of excitement thrummed through Mackenzie's veins. He tasted good. Clean. So masculine. If it was possible, the kiss was even better than what she had imagined it would be.

When Mackenzie finally pulled back, she was breathing heavily. She fluttered her eyelashes, trying to regain her equilibrium.

"Sorry," he said, loosening his grip, but not releasing her. "I just had to do that. It's all I've been thinking about all day." His tone was sexy and utterly tantalizing.

She laughed, feeling nervous and excited at the same time. "It's okay," she confessed. "I've been thinking about the same thing all day." She opened the bag of popcorn and poured it into a big bowl.

"So why didn't you want to go out with me tonight?" He picked up the glasses and followed her into the living room.

"I had things to do."

He eyed her.

"And . . . I didn't know if this was what I wanted." She sat down on the couch in front of the TV.

He sat beside her. "Can I ask why?"

She set the popcorn bowl between them and reached for the remote. "You're asking too many questions, Ben. Men don't ask questions about what women think, certainly not what they feel. Most of them don't care."

He scooped up a handful of popcorn, looking sheepish. "To be honest, I do try to avoid such topics. Or at least I have in the past." He tossed a piece of popcorn into his mouth. "Too messy."

"Makes it hard to make your getaway, doesn't it?"

He smirked. "Something tells me that you and I are a lot alike. Been through a lot of the same things."

"You'd be amazed," she muttered under her breath.

He reached for more popcorn. "Sorry?"

She shook her head, chuckling as she reached for the remote. She knew she needed to tell Ben that they had known each other in high school, but her opportunity seemed to have passed. Besides, it was time for the movie to start.

For the next two hours Mackenzie and Ben sat side by side on the couch, eating popcorn and licorice, drinking soda, and watching one of their favorite movies. Howard reluctantly relinquished his place beside Mackenzie on the couch and rested on the floor in front of the TV.

As the credits rolled, Mackenzie turned to Ben. "Thanks for coming," she said. It had been so nice having him here, sharing in the companionship of the evening. She'd felt so lonely since she moved to Land's End to be with Nana. "I didn't think I wanted to go out," she tried to explain, "but by the time I got home, I guess I just didn't feel like being alone."

Ben slipped his arm around her shoulder. The room was dark except for the light of the TV as an advertisement for a sports car flashed on the screen. Howie made doggy sounds in his sleep.

"Something wrong?" Ben asked. "I mean other than the fact that you've just started a new business and you're petrified you're going to go under, you're short a work crew and doing a job yourself, and you've got a big benefit shindig to pull off in two weeks?"

She sighed. "Actually, it's my grandmother. She's in a nursing home—Westview—and she's not doing well." Her eyes suddenly felt scratchy, surprising her. She thought she had done all the crying she ever would for Nana. That was all she had done the first month after she came back to Land's End.

"You didn't tell me you had family here." He took her hand. "So she's very ill?"

Mackenzie nodded. "She had a stroke a few months back. That was when I decided to move to Land's End and start my business. To be with her. She still breathes on her own but she doesn't seem to know what's going on around her. She doesn't even recognize me. Now she's not eating well."

He rubbed her shoulder. "I'm sorry to hear that. She's lucky to have you to worry about her."

Mackenzie glanced up at Ben. He was a good listener. And that was such a nice thing for him to say. "Thanks," she whispered.

"You're welcome."

This time, as he leaned over to kiss her, she met him halfway. Suddenly she craved affection. Human touch. She needed to be kissed.

Ben's mouth met hers, warm and searching. He applied just the right amount of pressure and Mackenzie curled tighter against him as the kiss deepened.

Mackenzie molded her body to his, and he eased his hand beneath her sweatshirt. His touch was hot on her bare belly.

She moaned softly as he slid his finger upward and stroked her breast. She had taken off her bra hours ago, after she'd arrived home.

Mackenzie didn't know if she laid back on the couch or if Ben eased her back. It didn't really matter. The kisses, the caresses, they were all by mutual consent.

"You're so beautiful," Ben whispered, rubbing her nipple with the rough pad of his thumb.

Fingers of pleasure rippled through Mackenzie's

entire body. It had been a long time since a man had touched her. Longer since she had felt anything in response. In the last months with her professor, sex had gotten monotonous, almost mechanical. But this . . . there was nothing mechanical about Ben Gordon's lovemaking. He was a master. And it wasn't just the way he touched her; he was a good kisser. He was gentle, unhurried, teasing. And he didn't just kiss her mouth. He kissed her neck, her earlobes, the hollow of her throat. As he caressed her, he didn't just concentrate on her bare breasts; he stroked her belly, her shoulders, and her back beneath the sweatshirt.

Mackenzie's thoughts drifted as they kissed again and again, as her breath came faster and her blood seemed to rush through her veins. She pulled her shirt off and let it fall to the floor. His bare skin and the crisp hair on his chest felt so wonderful beneath her fingertips. This was how she had imagined making love with the right man would be.

She could feel that familiar tingle in her groin.

She wanted him.

She could have him.

He slid her sweatshirt upward and lowered his head. She could already imagine the feel of his warm, wet mouth on her breast, but—

"Ben," she whispered, covering his hand with hers. "Ben, please. Stop."

He stopped immediately and lifted his head.

"What?" he murmured huskily. "What's wrong, Mackenzie? Don't you like—"

"Yes, I like it," she moaned sitting up, pushing her sweatshirt down. "But I can't do this. I won't—" She didn't mean to be a tease; that hadn't been her intention. But she couldn't go through with it.

Ben was breathing heavily, too. There was a thin sheen of perspiration on his forehead. "What's the matter?" he asked.

Mackenzie got up and pushed down her sweatshirt. She could still taste his mouth on hers, feel his hand on her tingling breast. "I can't do this," she said again. She made herself look at him. "Not with anyone but my husband. . . ."

Eight

Ben wasn't thinking clearly. Her kisses, her hands on his bare chest, she had made him forget who he was. Nothing mattered but Mackenzie and her sweet lips . . . and now she was saying something about her husband?

He was completely confused. She was married? He'd done a lot of lousy things in his life when it came to women, but he'd never stooped that low.

No, she couldn't be married. Could she?

He looked at her. Please don't let her be married, he thought, feeling uneasy in the pit of his stomach.

"You . . . you have husband?" he asked, trying to appear calm on the outside. His heart was pounding, his palms were sweaty and his groin . . . he felt as if he were going to explode.

She backed up, bumped into the coffee table between the couch and the TV, and went around it to put more distance between them.

The dog lifted his head off the carpet and watched his flustered master carefully.

"No, I don't have a husband," she said.

She seemed as shaken as Ben felt. When he had come here tonight, making love to Mackenzie hadn't really been his intention. Maybe for the first time since puberty, sex hadn't been the first and only thing on his mind. Companionship had. But five more minutes and he was pretty certain they would have been naked on the floor.

"You don't?" he breathed, relieved but still concerned. He did like Mackenzie. *Really* liked her, and the idea that she might be attached to someone else scared him. "Separated? Divorced? What?" He spread his arms, trying not to sound too demanding, but needing to know.

She wrapped her arms around her waist as if she wanted to protect herself and suddenly he felt like a heel. She looked so vulnerable at that moment that all he wanted to do was put his arms around her.

"I don't understand," he said more gently. "You said you couldn't—you said only with your *husband.*"

"That's not what I meant," she said miserably.

He could tell she was close to tears. He grabbed his sweatshirt off the floor and stood up to pull it over his head. To his surprise, he was trembling all over. She'd really gotten him worked up, but he was filled with emotion as well, something he wasn't used to. She was upset and it was his fault. "Mackenzie, it's all right," he said, trying to soothe her. He wasn't good at this; he didn't know what to say to calm her. He only knew he wanted to. "It's all right," he repeated lamely.

"It's not all right. I shouldn't have asked you over."

He understood what she meant, that she felt guilty,

as though he might have thought she was leading him on. What kind of jerk did she think he was?

The kind he had been. Had been, maybe as recently as five minutes ago. "Mackenzie, having a man over for popcorn and a movie doesn't entitle him to have sex with you," he said.

She drew her lips taut. "I'm really sorry, it's just that. . . ." She glanced away toward the light of the kitchen, then back at him. "It's just that I moved to Land's End for a lot of reasons, not just because of my grandmother. I wanted to start a new life."

He stood across the coffee table from her, listening. His heart was still beating irregularly, but at least he wasn't trembling anymore. He was thinking more clearly—with his head and not the body part men relied on too often.

"I've dated a lot of men over the years," she explained. "And none of it came to anything. None of them were particularly good for me." He understood exactly what she meant. That was the same conclusion he had come to this summer when he'd come up with that nutty Bachelors Inc. idea. He just hadn't been able to say it aloud.

She took a deep breath, her voice shaky. "I had some long-term relationships, all that I thought were going to be permanent. I'm not saying I slept around, but I have to admit that I gave myself completely to those men I loved. I thought they loved me, and that marriage was a possibility." She brushed her fingertips across her left breast. "Those men hurt me and I hurt myself by letting them hurt me."

She was a brave woman to come right out and

admit that, to herself, to a man. Ben admired her guts.

"So." She took another breath, calmer now. "When I moved here, I decided I needed to make some changes. I wasn't even looking to go out with anyone, but if I did—"

"You didn't intend to have sex with them."

"Exactly."

"Not ever again, unless you were married."

It sounded like a sentence of some sort to him. She nodded.

Both were quiet for a moment.

Ben gathered his thoughts, running one hand through his hair. Inside he was feeling such a crazy mix of emotions, many he wasn't familiar with. "Well, I won't say I'm not disappointed."

Thankfully, that made her give a little laugh.

"But I admire you for your conviction." He liked the fact that she was nearly as tall as he was. She met his gaze head-on; she was meeting him head-on. "I mean that." And he did. He respected her more at this moment than he had when he walked in her door.

"I just didn't want you to think I meant to lead you on," she said letting her arms drop to her sides as she relaxed a little. "When I invited you over, it really was just for popcorn and a movie."

"I know that." He picked his coat up off the chair where he'd left it. She obviously wanted him to leave, which was all right with him. What he needed right now was the proverbial cold shower and time to think. "How about if I go home now?" He started for the door. "I'll let myself out."

But at the door, he turned back. He felt strangely

at odds. He didn't want to leave Mackenzie. Even knowing he wasn't going to get this beautiful woman into the sack—ever—he still didn't want to leave her. "Hey," he called to her.

"Yeah?"

Her long, blond hair was tousled, her green eyes intense. She was still gorgeous to him, but in a slightly different kind of way. Something about the forbidden, maybe? Zack and his penchant for psychological analysis would have a ball with him right now.

"I'm invited to a poker game tomorrow night at my partner's house. Want to come?"

"Guys night out?" she questioned, looking doubtful.

"Nah. These guys are thoroughly attached. Both recently married. You'd like their wives. You'd like them."

"And you want me to go with you, even—"

"I want you to come," he said. "I wouldn't ask you if I didn't."

She offered him the cutest hint of a smile. "Okay."

"Okay?" He felt as if he was a kid again. How long had it been since he was excited about the prospect of a date?

"Okay, I'll come."

"Great! I'll pick you up at 6:45? Unless, of course, you want to drive yourself." He gestured with one hand, the same hand he had just stroked her breast with. "Because I'm all right with that."

"Come get me," she said, still not moving from that spot on the carpet in front of the TV.

"See you tomorrow night."

Ben let himself out the door and hurried through the cold darkness to his car. He fumbled with the keys and let himself in.

A date? He'd made another date?

He had no idea what he was doing. Why was he pursuing Mackenzie, especially after what had just happened? What did he possibly think he was going to get out of the relationship, he, a man who had given up on male/female relationships?

Ben started the engine and pulled out of the apartment-house parking lot. He had no idea where he thought this thing with Mackenzie was going, or where he wanted it to go. All he knew was that he had this strange feeling he couldn't live without her.

Mackenzie watched Ben pull out of the parking lot before she let the curtain fall over the cold windowpane. Her hands were still trembling.

She couldn't believe she'd almost gone to bed with him. The first real date she'd had in months, the first opportunity and she'd almost blown it.

But she hadn't blown it. She couldn't believe she had been able to stop. She had wanted Ben Gordon, really wanted him, both mentally and physically.

Then she'd come up with that ridiculously cliched, out-of-date declaration that she would only do *that* with her husband.

She had put herself in a dangerous position for a woman. He could have forced her.

He could have tried to convince her otherwise,

plying her with his warm tongue and knowledge-
able hands.

He could have laughed.

She felt her mouth stretch into a silly grin. He
hadn't done any of those things. He'd acted honor-
ably—a strange word to apply to the Casanova she'd
once known. But, bless his heart, Ben had been so
gallant about it. Like some kind of old-fashioned
hero from a Saturday afternoon movie.

He was a nice guy. A really nice guy. And she
liked him way too much.

She walked away from the window. The trembling
of desire had passed, but she still felt shaky all over.
She turned off the TV and then grabbed the dirty
glasses and popcorn bowl off the coffee table to
carry to the kitchen.

The way the night ended could have been labeled a date disaster, but thanks to Ben, it hadn't
been. He'd been so nice to her, so understanding.
And he'd actually asked her out again. Why she
wasn't sure. He knew now that he wasn't going to
get a tumble in the sheets with her.

So maybe he just asked her out because he liked
her.

Mackenzie felt her face grow warm at the
thought. Could it possibly be that the playboy Ben
was lonely, too? Looking for companionship as well?

Soul mates? she wondered. Then she laughed
aloud. A mutual love for pineapple and Canadian
bacon did not add up to soul mates.

Howie trotted into the kitchen.

"What's the matter, boy? Did I scare you, laughing like a crazy woman?" She placed the dirty

dishes in the sink and leaned over to scratch his back.

"So what did you think of him? Did you like Bennett?"

They said dogs knew things people didn't, that sometimes they were better judges of character.

Howie wagged his tail enthusiastically.

"Does that mean yes, or does that mean your back was itchy and now you feel better?"

The dog whined in response.

"Okay," she said, giving him a pat. "Let's go out for a quick walk and then it's off to bed."

Howie ran to the door and dragged his leash out of a basket against the wall.

Grabbing her coat off a pegboard on the wall, she followed him. "I think I've spent enough time thinking about Ben Gordon for one day, don't you?"

Enough time thinking about him, for sure. But that didn't mean she couldn't dream about him.

At seven the next evening Ben escorted Mackenzie up the steps and onto the porch of Owen and Abby's rambling Victorian home.

"What a beautiful house," she murmured, running her hand up the painted banister.

"Abby grew up here," Ben explained. "I guess I've been here a million times."

Mackenzie was nervous about seeing Ben's friends. She had known them back in high school, too. What if someone remembered her? If Ben hadn't, she rationalized, no one else would.

She probably should have told him the truth on

the way over, but they were having such a nice conversation. He had asked her about her hobbies, and she'd told him she liked to paint pictures as well as walls. He seemed genuinely interested. He wanted to come back to the apartment to get a better look at the work that hung on her walls.

Ben rang the doorbell, but he didn't wait for anyone to answer. Obviously, he felt at home here. "In the kitchen!" a woman called from the back of the house as they stepped in the front door. The sound of laughter rang off the dark, Victorian-paneled walls.

A huge black, white and brown dog came bounding to the door.

"Oh, my goodness, he's huge," Mackenzie exclaimed, holding out both arms to the lumbering dog. He had a big head, a short muzzle and large floppy ears. "What is he, a Saint Bernard?"

"A Bernese mountain dog."

Mackenzie leaned over and petted his broad head.

The dog chuffed with excitement and looked at her with the big brown eyes of a newfound friend. He must have smelled Howie on her hands and clothes.

"His name is Edgar," Ben said, starting down the hall. "Come on, I want you to meet everyone else."

Mackenzie would rather have stayed in the hall with the dog, but at this point, if she was in for a penny, she was in for a pound. She rose and the dog followed.

They passed a wide, polished staircase on the right. A room on the left was dark, but she could make out a desk and architectural easels. This had to be where Owen worked. The kitchen was off the rear of the front hall.

" 'Evening all," Ben said. "I want you meet Mackenzie."

The kitchen was brightly lit and had a beautiful hardwood floor and painted, windowed cabinets that showed a collection of nineteenth-century porcelain. A round oak table dominated the center of the room. Everyone was already seated around the table ready to play poker.

"Nice to have you with us." A man with shoulder-length hair pulled back in a ponytail rose. "I'm Zack and this is my wife, Kayla."

Mackenzie nodded and smiled. She remembered Zack well. His family had been the resident hippies in town. He'd always been a little different from everyone else, and she had admired him for being comfortable with being different.

There was no sign of recognition on his face when he nodded pleasantly.

"Great to have you with us," Kayla said, shuffling cards. She was a pretty, athletic-looking woman with shoulder-length hair and warm eyes. The physician.

"Glad Ben brought you," a clean-cut looking man said, rising to his feet and offering his hand.

Owen. She remembered him. He'd always been such a nice guy but more of a follower than a leader, unlike Ben.

"I'm Owen, and this is my wife Abby." He ran his hand playfully over her abdomen. "And my son—"

Mackenzie shook his hand.

"Or daughter." Abby smiled warmly. "Thanks for

coming. Have a seat. Can I get you anything to drink? We've got beer and soda."

Mackenzie sat directly across from Abby in one of the two vacant chairs. "I'm fine right now. Thanks."

Abby leaned across the table, studying her. "Hey, I know you from somewhere."

Mackenzie stiffened.

Ben was getting a beer out of the refrigerator. "She's pretty new in town. Just started that painting business Sayer and Sons." He gave her a reassuring smile. He really liked these people and on the ride over, he had made it obvious that he hoped she would like them, too.

"Maybe we've run into each other at the gym or the grocery store," Mackenzie said, wishing she'd worn a mask. She should have known Abby would recognize her. Men could be blockheads about these kinds of things, but women never forgot other women. It didn't matter how many years or pounds had come or gone.

"No, I haven't seen you around town." Abby shook her finger. "Where did you go to school?"

"Temple University."

Abby shook her head, wracking her brain. "No, before that. You're from here, aren't you? From Land's End."

Now Mackenzie wanted to climb under the table with the dog.

"You didn't go to school here," Ben said. He stared at her, probably realizing that he hadn't asked her where she was from and she hadn't offered the information. "Did you?"

"That's it!" Abby slapped the table. "I knew it!

You went to school with us. I remember you were in my chemistry II class." She frowned. "But you didn't go by Mackenzie." Her eyes grew round with discovery. "Margaret! That's it! You were Margaret Sayer!"

Ben turned to look at her, his beer poised in midair, and Mackenzie thought for a moment that she was going to be sick.

Nine

"That's ridiculous, Abby," Ben said, lowering the beer. "I was in your chemistry class, which would mean—"

He obviously hadn't noticed or didn't comprehend the stricken look on Mackenzie's face. She swallowed and glanced up. "It would mean we were in class together."

"Sheesh, Ben! What a dolt. Yes, she was in your class." Abby went to the refrigerator to get more ice for her soda.

All three men stared at Mackenzie, making her self-conscious. They were obviously attempting unsuccessfully to remember her.

Ben smirked. "Come on. You guys are pulling my leg. Did you set this up ahead of time?" He took a sip of his beer. "I would certainly remember a six-foot tall blonde in one of my classes, even after all these years."

Mackenzie eyed him, annoyed and not certain why. "Not if she wasn't six-feet tall or a blonde . . . *yet.*"

Ben stared blankly.

Abby took her seat again. "Think, Ben. Tallest

girl in the class. Sat in the back. Probably the smartest student in the class and she was a junior."

"I feel silly," Ben confessed to Mackenzie, "but I honestly don't remember you."

A part of Mackenzie wanted to just get up and leave. All those feelings of insecurity she had experienced in high school were tumbling back. These had been the "in" people back then. Abby was a cheerleader, Zack the resident math geek/genius. Ben was the captain of the soccer team, and everyone's dream date; Owen was everyone's best friend. And then there had been Margaret Sayer, the girl trying to remain as inconspicuous as a five-foot-nine, one-hundred-and-seventy-five pound girl could.

"There wouldn't be any reason for you to remember me," she told Ben, meeting his gaze head-on. "I was unmemorable at the time."

He frowned, still thinking. "Okay, I'm a dolt. I'm still not following you.

"I was fat," she said flatly.

Abby scrunched up her nose. "Oh, you were not."

"I was fat, my hair was mousy, and I wore thick glasses."

"I clearly remember that everyone wanted to be your lab partner." Abby pointed a finger. "Ben was the lucky guy." She shot him a look across the table. "I can't believe you didn't remember your lab partner." She shook her head. "Men."

Mackenzie didn't know what to say. She really didn't want to get into this conversation now, if ever. What was the sense in rehashing things that happened twenty years ago? The thing was, she didn't know how to get out of it gracefully.

"Look, this blast from the past is all very charming," Kayla said, dealing the cards, "but are we here to play poker or what?"

Mackenzie glanced at Kayla, flashing a look of gratitude. *Rescued.* Mackenzie knew Kayla understood how she was feeling right now. She smiled and Mackenzie was certain she had made a friend.

Thankfully, everyone took the hint and let the subject drop. They then proceeded to play poker for an hour—dealer's choice. Mackenzie was actually up a dollar and a half when they broke for a bathroom break and to stretch their legs.

Mackenzie had just refilled her soda glass with ice when Ben grabbed her hand and pulled her into the dark laundry room just off the kitchen.

"Did we really know each other in high school?" he asked. His tone reflected a slight hint of disbelief but a willingness to be objective. Maybe even to grovel if necessary.

Mackenzie liked a man who knew when to grovel. "I'm afraid so."

"And you knew it the first time we met, I suppose?"

"Women don't forget the best-looking guys they went through puberty adoring," she said tartly. "They usually take those faces to their graves."

He moved closer to her, the darkness of the room enveloping them. The room smelled of laundry detergent and dog food.

Ben laced his fingers through hers and held tightly to her hand. "Why didn't you tell me?"

He was being so nice. Trying hard to be understanding.

"I don't know. I should have; I'm sorry." She looked away and then back at him. "I guess a part of me wanted you to remember me." She paused. "And a part was afraid you would."

"Mackenzie, this is silly. That was a long time ago and we were kids."

"I was fat, Ben." She met his gaze. "Don't you know what that means to a woman? I was awkward and I felt ugly."

He smoothed her hair in a tender caress. "You know, I do remember you now, and not like that."

"No?"

"I remember that you were quiet, studious."

"Fat?" she asked. "You don't remember the fat part?"

He shook his head. "No, I don't remember thinking that, though I do recall that you were taller than we were." He gave a little laugh. "And very intimidating."

It was her turn to laugh. A woman could never know for sure when a man was lying to her to make her feel better, but her gut instinct told her he was being honest in his recollections. "Me, intimidating?"

"Why not? You certainly are now."

She was taken aback. "I am? Why—just because I'm five-foot-eleven in my stocking feet?"

"Because you're a five-foot-eleven woman with a hell of an attitude." He leaned forward and kissed her. "And I mean that as a compliment."

She smiled up at him. "You know, that may be the nicest thing anyone has ever said about me."

"Hey, you guys! Ben! Mackenzie! No hanky-panky in my laundry room!" Owen hollered from the kitchen.

"Yeah," Zack chimed in. "That room is only meant for hanky-panky for us married folk!"

Everyone laughed.

Mackenzie felt her cheeks grow warm. "We'd better go back in before they send the troops in after us." She started to pull away, but he tugged on her hand.

"A kiss first?" he whispered.

Mackenzie's thoughts and emotions were all in a jumble. Ben was being so damned nice. Why? He knew he wasn't getting her into his bed. Under that playboy exterior could he possibly be this chivalrous?

Mackenzie drew close to him, looking directly into his eyes. In her loafers, she was as tall as he was. She pressed her mouth to his.

Ben's kiss was warm, gentle, but with a trace of excitement. He tasted of light beer and the hint of a man who could be trusted. Maybe even loved.

Mackenzie pulled away, startled by the thought. "Come on," she said, and pulled him into the light of the kitchen.

Zack was already dealing the cards. "Five card stud," he announced. "Nothing wild."

"Purist." Ben accused as he pulled out Mackenzie's chair for her, then sat beside her.

The men laughed at the accusation. "In case you haven't noticed," Abby said to Mackenzie, "nothing has changed with these boys since high school. The theory that we all grow up"—she eyed Mackenzie over the edge of her fanned cards—"is untrue, at least in this case."

Mackenzie picked up her cards. "Actually, I was thinking how nice it is that you've all remained friends." She glanced cautiously at the others. "I've always been a bit of a loner, so I guess I'm a little envious. It must be nice not having to always be giving background stuff; you all know each other's history."

"Well, knowing each other's business since you were ten can be trying at times," Abby said. "But you're right. We are lucky. And whether these guys will admit it or not, they know it."

"Friends since they've been in diapers or not," Kayla piped up, "I have to say—as a recent outsider, now on the inside—they've all been extremely kind to me."

Kayla smiled warmly at Zack and Mackenzie watched with fascination as he smiled back. They were obviously very much in love and it was funny, but she enjoyed just being in the presence of couples who cared that much about each other. It gave Mackenzie hope, for herself, maybe for the entire human race.

"Hey, speaking of good friends," Ben said. "Kayla, I was wondering if you might do me a little favor."

Kayla laid two cards face down and took the new ones from the deck that Zack offered. "No, Ben. The answer is no."

Abby started to laugh. Owen and Zack sniggered.

Mackenzie thought she knew what he was getting at, too. He was still trying to get out of decorating the Christmas trees himself.

"What do you mean?" Ben said innocently. "I haven't even asked you the favor yet. How do you know what I was going to say?"

"I know what you're going to say, and the answer is no." Kayla eyed Mackenzie, a look of amusement on her face. "Face it, being the desperate man that you are, you sold yourself for a date, and now you have to pay the piper."

Ben groaned and slumped in his seat. "I can't believe my friends are going to fail me now, just when I need them most."

Mackenzie grabbed a pretzel from the bag on the table. "So"—she munched the pretzel—"do you have an idea what the themes of your trees are going to be?"

Everyone burst into laughter, and Mackenzie felt more like a part of something than she'd ever felt before.

The next time they took a break from the game, Kayla asked Abby if she'd started on the nursery and all three women traipsed up the stairs to ooh and aah over the newly painted room. The three men remained in the kitchen and whipped up some nachos.

As Ben grated the cheddar cheese, he thought about the way Abby and Owen, and Zack and Kayla behaved together. He had to confess, he was envious, just as Mackenzie had said she was envious of the friendships they shared. Ben had never thought a long-term relationship was for him or him for it, but watching the other two couples tonight was making him question himself.

While Owen went out to the laundry room to get

some tomatoes out of the spare fridge, Zack remained in the kitchen with Ben to chop an onion.

"Seems like married life agrees with you," Ben said, trying to sound causal, but knowing it came out awkwardly. He wasn't as good as Zack was when it came to expressing himself and his feelings. He tended to keep things inside, especially when it came to his own emotions.

Zack looked up from the onion, his eyes teary. "Best thing that ever happened to me." He grinned like a fool. "I love her. Every inch of her. Love her to death."

"So, no regrets?" Ben elbowed him. "Buddy to buddy?"

"Absolutely none. Getting married and doing it right away was the best thing for us. We've already settled into a nice routine at home and Savannah is definitely happier."

Zack had been having some problems with his daughter earlier in the school year. Nothing big, just poor grades and some misbehavior, but Ben knew Zack had been very concerned. Apparently, all the little girl had really needed was another female in the house, one that cared about her.

"And you don't feel as if you've lost . . . I don't know . . . some of your freedom?" Ben pressed.

"What freedom? No, I can't leave my underwear on the floor because she'll throw it in my face, and because I'm outnumbered by females, I now leave the toilet seat down, but other than that"—Zack shrugged—"I don't have any less freedom. I go where I want, when I want. So does Kayla. But mostly I just want to be with her." Zack gave him a silly grin.

Owen returned to the kitchen, carrying some tomatoes and another two-liter bottle of diet soda.

"Our perpetual bachelor is getting contemplative on us," Zack said, motioning with the knife. "Wants to know if the phrase 'happily married' has any merit."

"Well," Owen set the soda on the counter, "I can honestly say I'm happier than I've ever been in my life. Abby and I have had some hard times, but now that we're beyond that, I know this is what's right for me. For both of us."

The cheese grated, Ben passed Zack the bowl. He wanted to ask another question, but wasn't sure how to phrase it. He didn't want to insult his buddies, or more importantly, their wives. After stalling, he just blurted it out. "And what about the sex?"

Owen tossed him the three tomatoes one by one as he and Zack exchanged looks. "What about it? It's great! Knock down, knock out, if it was any more perfect, I'd fall over dead."

Ben laughed as he caught the tomatoes and began to juggle them. "I don't need the gory details. But you know what I mean?"

"You mean is it a problem realizing I'm never going to make love with any other woman but Kayla the rest of my life?"

"I suppose that's what I'm asking," Ben said sheepishly.

"Nope. Not a problem. It's what I want. I honestly can't imagine ever being with anyone else but Kayla."

"Ditto," Owen said. "With Abby of course, not Kayla."

Zack laughed.

One by one, Ben dropped the tomatoes onto the counter. He didn't know what had made him ask his buddies these questions. He just needed to know.

Somehow, Owen and Zack seemed to sense that he didn't want to explore the reasons why he was talking crazy like this. And being the good friends that they were, they knew instinctively, as all men do, how to skirt a serious issue.

"So what kind of team do you think the Orioles will have next spring?" Owen asked diplomatically.

The men were in a heated discussion over the ball club's pitching when the women came downstairs from the nursery and started up the poker game again.

It was after eleven when Ben and Mackenzie said their good-byes and headed out into the frosty night. A few flakes of snow drifted in the cold breeze as they crossed the driveway to Ben's car. "Beautiful night," she breathed.

"Incredible."

Ben opened the car door for her, and she climbed in. They rode home in comfortable silence, neither seeming to feel the need for idle chatter. In a way, Mackenzie was reluctant to go home. What if this was it? What if this date, one he'd made to prove he was an okay guy, was to be their last? After all, she couldn't blame Ben. A lot of men his age wouldn't date a woman whom they knew they weren't going to get sex out of.

Like a gentleman, Ben walked Mackenzie to her door. She wanted to ask him in just to extend the evening a few more minutes, but she didn't. She knew it wouldn't be right. She smiled. "Listen, thanks for tonight and I'm sorry about not telling you." She smoothed the collar of his jacket. "You know, about us having gone to school together."

He lifted one shoulder, his hands stuffed in his coat pockets. "Not a big deal. I was surprised, that's all. Felt a little foolish, maybe. I mean, Abby recognized you the minute you walked in. She's right, I am a dolt."

She smiled. "You're not a dolt." She nodded. "Okay, maybe a little bit of one, but that's what makes you so appealing—in a doltish kind of way."

He grinned at her silly joke. "Listen, I better go. Want me to give Howie a quick walk around the block?"

"Thanks, but I'll do it. I like getting a little air before I go to bed. Helps me sleep."

He pulled his hands out of his pockets, seeming not to quite know what to do. She knew he was thinking about the proverbial good-night kiss. She was thinking about it too.

"Well, good night," he said, surprising her by making no move toward her. In a second, he would turn away.

If he wasn't going to kiss her, she was going to kiss him. Mackenzie leaned toward him, and he immediately grabbed her around the waist. He wasn't rough, but he was forceful enough for her to know it wasn't that he hadn't wanted to kiss her, only that he'd wanted to do the right thing.

Mackenzie opened her mouth, reveling in the taste and feel of his tongue as it passed between her lips. A delicious, familiar tightness formed in her belly as he kissed her breathless. She still wanted him, he still wanted her, and there was no doubt about that.

When Ben stepped back, they were both breathing heavily. He stroked her cheek before releasing her. "So, you need to know Wednesday about the trees?"

"Wednesday," she breathed, not sure she could speak in whole sentences quite yet. The depth of the emotion that had accompanied his kiss still had her unsteady.

"By Wednesday for sure, then." He started to back away. "Good night."

Mackenzie watched him go down the hall toward the elevator. He didn't say anything else about a date, or even that he would call her, but she guessed that meant he would talk to her.

She unlocked her door and slipped inside.

The minute Ben pulled into the driveway, he knew something was wrong. The house was dark, the porch lights still on just the way he had left them when he went to pick up Mackenzie. His father wasn't home, yet he should have been back hours ago.

Ben let himself quickly into the house. Not bothering to take off his coat, he hurried down the hall. He opened his father's bedroom door. Certain no one was there, he flipped on the light. The single bed was neatly made. No Dad.

Ben went back downstairs to the answering machine. Maybe he'd left a message and needed a ride home. Ben had told him where he would be. He should have called Zack's house if he needed a ride home, but his father was getting more forgetful than he used to be.

Pushing aside his fear, Ben hit the PLAY button on the answering machine and played back the messages. The first was from a potential client. The second was a woman's voice. . . .

"Ben . . . um, this is Myrtle, Myrtle Atkins, um, your father's friend."

Her voice sounded emotional.

"Ben, you need to come right to the hospital when you get this message." Myrtle gave a sniff. She was obviously trying to hold back tears and leave a comprehensible message. "He's had a heart attack, dear."

Ben stood immobilized by shock for a moment. Of course he knew these kinds of things happened. But Max had just had a physical exam a month ago. "Fit as a fiddle," he'd said, quoting the doctor.

A heart attack. That meant he could die.

Ben ran for the door, not bothering to shut off the lights. As he raced toward his car, he fumbled for his cell phone in his coat pocket. It was strange, but there was only one person he needed to speak to right this minute.

Inside the car, he started the engine and then punched Mackenzie's phone number.

If this response card is missing, call us at 1-888-345-BOOK.

Be sure to visit our website at www.kensingtonbooks.com

PLACE
STAMP
HERE

Ten

Ben hurried through the sliding glass doors of the emergency waiting room and approached the reception desk. A woman peered over the edge of her horn-rimmed glasses at him. "May I help you?" Her voice was so mechanical that it startled him.

"Um, yes. My name is Ben Gordon." He spoke calmly, though his heart was pounding and he felt as if he wasn't getting any oxygen. "My father, Max Gordon, was apparently brought in with a possible heart attack."

She rolled her eyes downward to the paperwork on the desk in front of her and peered at the entries from below the rim of the glasses. "Yes, he was admitted, sir. At 9:57 this evening."

That was almost two hours ago. All this time and Ben hadn't known. He immediately felt a wave of guilt but checked it. How could he have known? Myrtle wouldn't have had any idea where he was, and Max had obviously not been in any condition to tell her.

Ben pressed his palms to the counter. "Can you tell me if he's all right?"

"Have a seat please, and I'll let someone know you're here. You'll be called."

"I just want to know if my dad is alive," Ben snapped, his fingertips going white as he pressed harder on the reception counter.

The receptionist eyed his hands sternly.

He pulled away.

"Patient status is not provided to reception," she droned. "Please have a seat. I'll let the attending physician know you're here."

He started to say something else and the woman glared, directly through the lenses of her glasses this time. Now she meant business. Ben swallowed his words and turned away. He'd give Robot Woman five minutes, then he was storming the place.

He walked over to the arena of cushioned chairs where patients and their families waited. A TV was mounted on a stand near the ceiling in the corner of the room; a late-night talk show host was interviewing a man with a pet iguana on a leash. Ben was too nervous to sit so he just paced, taking care not to walk in front of the TV. A woman sat in one of the chairs reading an old *Newsweek*, a child asleep in the chair beside her. Other than them, the room was empty.

Ben wondered where Myrtle was. Had she gone home? That would surely mean his father was doing okay. Or that he was dead, he thought morbidly.

No, he couldn't think this way. Bad vibes, Zack would say.

Zack. Ben had been so nervous that he'd been afraid to use his cell phone and drive at the same time. He should call Zack and Owen now. He'd expect them to call him if one of their parents was ill.

Ben pulled his cell phone from his coat pocket and hit the first digit—

"Excuse me, sir," came the robot receptionist's voice. "You can't use that here. You'll have to use the pay phone." She pointed with one bony finger toward the bank of public phones on the opposite wall.

Nazi receptionist, Ben thought, clearing his phone. He tucked it into his pocket and walked toward the pay phones. He doubted he had any change.

The pneumatic door opened behind him, and Ben heard his name called.

"Ben, you okay?"

Mackenzie rushed over and a strange sense of peace came over Ben. She put her arms around him, almost as if they belonged to each other. "I'm so sorry," she whispered in his ear.

Ben hugged her back. The warm human contact felt good. He suddenly didn't feel so alone. No matter what happened with his father, he felt as if he could face it now.

"How is he?" She gazed into his eyes. She had obviously dressed quickly. Her hair was pulled back in a ponytail but messy. She'd probably already been in bed when he called. Despite her rumpled clothing and face scrubbed clean of makeup, she was still startlingly beautiful.

"I don't know how he is. No one will tell me anything."

She took a step back but kept one arm around his waist.

The automatic doors opened again and Kayla

rushed in. She looked as if she'd just come out of her pajamas too.

"Kayla!" The three met in the middle of the reception area. "How did you know to come?"

"I called her," Mackenzie said, tight-lipped. "I hope you don't mind, but I know she works here."

"Of course he doesn't mind." Kayla was straightforward and upbeat. "Now listen, let me run back, see how he is, and then I'll come right back out and get you."

"They already told me I had to wait." Ben glanced angrily in the receptionist's direction.

She was watching them with what could have been perceived as interest, if she hadn't been so utterly lacking in human characteristics.

"Oh, don't mind Rosy," Kayla pashawed. "She's our gatekeeper, keeps the wolves at bay." She rubbed Ben's arm. "It's her job, hon. Don't take it personally."

Ben threw up one hand. "But I can't even get her to tell me if he's still alive."

"Ben, listen to me." Kayla met his gaze, her voice calm, but commanding.

He listened.

"If your dad had passed away, they wouldn't have asked you to wait out here. We have a different protocol for deaths."

Ben nodded, swallowing back his bitter fear. That should make him feel better, he knew, but honestly he wouldn't feel better until he saw his dad, until he felt his warm, wrinkled hand in his.

Mackenzie clung to Ben's other arm. He didn't really need her for balance, but he felt better just feeling her there beside him.

"We'll wait right here," Mackenzie told Kayla, who was already headed for the entrance to the emergency-treatment rooms.

Kayla flashed a grim smile. "Sit tight. I'll be right back."

Kayla disappeared through the door and Ben watched it swing shut. "Thanks for calling her." He rubbed his forehead. "I didn't think of that. She's a doctor, of course. Why didn't I think to call her right away?"

Mackenzie led him to the chairs and sat down, pulling him down beside her. She held his hand. "I'm sure the doctors on call have everything under control here; I just thought you might feel better if Kayla took a look. If you need any interpretation, she might be helpful." She smoothed his hand in hers. "When my grandmother had the stroke, I was so bombarded by medical terms that, at first, I didn't understand half of what I was being told."

Ben nodded. "It was good she came. Kayla will give us the honest truth. We'll know where Pop stands for sure."

"I called Owen, too. He'll be here any minute. Zack stayed with his daughter, but said to call if you need him and he'd be right over."

The ER door opened and Ben sprang up. Kayla walked briskly toward them. He couldn't tell for sure what she was thinking or how his dad was, but he didn't think he was dead. She didn't have that kind of look on her face.

"He's okay, Ben," Kayla said. "He's being transferred to a room on the cardiac ward right now."

Ben swallowed. He could hear his heart beating hollowly in his ears. "He's going to be okay?"

"Well, obviously there's a problem. He had a minor heart attack, so something's up, but for now he's stable and alert."

"Can I see him?"

Kayla smiled. "I'll walk you up."

Mackenzie gave Ben's hand a squeeze and let go. "I'll stay here and wait for Owen."

Ben ran a hand through his hair. He wasn't even sure now why he called Mackenzie. What could she do? All he knew was that at that moment he had needed her. "I . . . I guess you could go home," he said, feeling fragmented. His thoughts were going in every direction. He was very emotional.

"I'll hang around a little longer. Get a cup of coffee." She flashed a grin. "What's a trip to the hospital without a cup of ladies' auxiliary coffee?"

"He's in Room 234," Kayla said. "Give us a few minutes to check on him, and then you come up and fetch Ben. He won't be able to stay long tonight."

Mackenzie winked. "See you in a few."

Kayla led Ben through the ER treatment hallway and down another hallway to an elevator marked Staff Only.

They stepped in and she punched the second-floor button. "Faster," she said. On the way up, she briefed him on Max's condition. He'd definitely had a heart attack and blockage was suspected. His father would have to have an angioplasty in the next few days, but the cardiologist on call seemed certain his father's chances at recovery were excellent.

When the elevator stopped, Kayla led him down a hall and through swinging glass doors. The limited visiting hours were posted on the door. "Two thirty-four, two thirty-four," Kayla repeated absently. "Here he is."

They entered a private room. Max was lying in a hospital bed, his eyes shut. Monitors beeped and clucked around him. Ben tried to remind himself of the positive outcome Kayla had predicted, but his dad looked so pale.

Myrtle, who appeared to have been dozing in a chair beside the bed, started and rose out of her seat. "Oh, thank goodness you're here." She flapped her hands. Myrtle was an attractive woman in her late sixties. She had a fashionable haircut and was dressed in a pair of khakis and a sweater. Like Ben's father, she wore her age well. "I hated to leave such a message, but I didn't know where you were and Max—" Her voice caught in her throat. "You understand, he couldn't tell me where you were."

Ben reached out and squeezed the woman's hand. "Thanks so much for staying with him until I could get here, Myrtle." Ben's mind still felt fuzzy, but he could see his father was okay, at least for the time being. He watched his father's chest rise and fall for a moment before he spoke to Myrtle again. "Um. It's really late. Can one of us give you a ride home?"

She fluttered her hands again. "No. I have my car. I followed the ambulance." She glanced at Max. "I'm just so relieved he didn't. . . ."

She didn't have to finish her sentence; Ben knew what she meant. Myrtle was glad he hadn't died. And at this moment, Ben was saying his own silent thank-yous.

"How about if I walk Myrtle down?" Kayla suggested. "Then I'll have a look-see at the charts and let you know your dad's status."

Ben turned back to his father's friend. "This is Kayla Burns. Dr. Kayla Burns," he corrected. It was funny, he rarely thought of Kayla as a doctor. She was just his buddy's wife. But at this moment, he was exceedingly thankful Zack had married one. "Zack Taylor's wife."

Myrtle shook Kayla's hand. "Oh, a lady doctor," she exclaimed, starting out of the room. "Your mother must be so proud."

Kayla gave Ben a little smile and escorted Myrtle the Turtle out of the room. Only after they were gone did Ben allow himself to approach his father's bed. Tentatively, he picked up his hand. It was cool to the touch.

A lump rose in Ben's throat. His father could have died. He still could and the thought frightened him to the core. If his father died, Ben would have no one. No family, at least. His sister was settled in Australia with her family, half a world away. Sure, he would still have Zack and Owen, but they had their own families. He loved those guys like they were his brothers, but as he held his father's hand, he realized this was different. Family was different.

Ben lowered himself into the chair beside the bed. The room was quiet except for the beep and hum of the monitors. An automatic blood pressure cuff whined as it took his father's blood pressure and then exhaled with the moan of a tired man.

Max's eyes fluttered and Ben leaned closer to the bed. His father seemed to be coming to.

Max moved his head and gave Ben a weak smile. "Son."

Ben exhaled. "You gave us quite a scare, Pop."

"Didn't win a basket either," Max grumbled.

Ben leaned closer. "What, Dad?" He wondered if the hospital had given him some kind of drug that had befuddled him.

"A basket. One of those damned baskets!" He closed his eyes. "We went to Basket Bingo. I told Myrtle I'd win her one of those baskets. Now I guess I'll have to buy her one, full price."

Ben chuckled with relief. Same old Dad. For once, he was happy to hear him complain.

Max sounded very tired. "How'd you know I was here?"

"Myrtle left a message on the answering machine. I didn't get home until a little while ago, though. Then I came right away."

Max pulled his hand from Ben's and pushed the hair off his forehead. "Have a nice evening?"

"Very nice."

"Like that Amazon painter, don't you?"

Ben glanced away. When he thought about Mackenize, his chest tightened. "I like her."

"So do something about it!" Max's voice was suddenly strong.

Ben met his father's gaze. "We can talk about this later."

"And what if there isn't a later, son?"

Ben immediately wondered if Max knew something about his condition that he didn't. Had Kayla been overly positive in her assessment?

Ben stood up and leaned over the bed. He smoothed the sheets as he tried to calm his father.

Surely, this upset couldn't be good for him. "Dad, Kayla says the heart attack wasn't bad. You're probably going to need an angioplasty, but they'll know more after some testing tomorrow."

"Anything could happen," he muttered. "Could die on the table. Die under the knife."

"They use a catheter and a balloon for an angioplasty, Pop. No knives."

"Could die anyway."

Ben could feel his hands tremble. "You could, but Kayla thinks it will be pretty routine, and you'll be fine." He tried to sound more positive than he felt. "She thinks you'll be home by the end of the week."

"Maybe, but even if I make it through this one, I'm not going to be around forever, you know." Max said matter-of-factly "And where will that leave you?"

Ben didn't like talking about this. He didn't want to think about it. He just couldn't imagine his father being gone. He couldn't imagine being alone in that house. "Pop—"

"Alone. Lonely," Max said. "That's where you'll be when I take my leave."

"Dad, you're not going anywhere. Not anytime soon, at least." Ben took his father's hand again, wondering if he ought to call a nurse. He wished Kayla would hurry up and come back. His father was making him nervous. What if he gave himself another heart attack?

"I think it's time you settled down, son. To hell with this bachelor nonsense. It's not what God made us for."

Ben glanced away, focusing on the darkness beyond the window. He didn't know what to say. He wanted to argue with his father, but somewhere inside he knew there was truth to what he said.

"Why don't you try to get some sleep?" Ben whispered, rubbing his father's hand. "We can talk about this tomorrow."

"Promise me you'll think about it!" Max met Ben's gaze.

Ben hated to see his father upset like this. "I'll think about it."

"Thank you." Max closed his eyes. "Now go on home and get some sleep. Don't forget to add food to the bird feeder before you come in the morning."

Ben squeezed his dad's hand and then let go. "Will do." For a minute he stood over his father. Max seemed to already have drifted off. "Love you, Pop," he whispered.

Ben ran into Mackenzie and Owen and Kayla in the hallway outside the door. "How is he?" Owen asked.

"Okay, I think. We'll know more tomorrow."

Mackenzie reached out and rubbed Ben's arm. He liked the attention. He needed the comfort.

Owen glanced around. "You want me to stay, buddy? I don't mind."

Ben glanced over his shoulder at Max's door. He could see his father sleeping peacefully. "No, I'm okay."

"You going to stay or go home?"

"I think I might have a cup of coffee, come back and check on him, and then go home for a few hours sleep if Kayla thinks that's okay." Ben waved. "But you go home and go to bed. You too, Kayla.

I appreciate you coming out in the middle of the night to check up on Dad for me."

Kayla rubbed Ben's shoulder. "I'm just glad I could be here for you."

Owen glanced at Mackenzie. "You staying or going?"

"I think I'll have a cup of coffee, too," she said quietly.

Owen glanced back at Ben. "You call me if anything happens, okay?"

Ben nodded. "You betcha."

"If there's a problem," Kayla said, "the nurses' station said they would call me. The best thing you can do now is go home and get some sleep."

The four rode down the elevator together. Owen and Kayla got off on the first floor and then Mackenzie and Ben rode down to the basement. There was a small coffee shop there open twenty-four hours a day.

Ben got them each a cup of coffee and they took chairs across from each other at a small table. Ben added some sugar to his coffee and stirred with a brown plastic stick.

"You okay?" she asked, studying him carefully. She drank her coffee black. A purist like Zack.

"I'm okay. I just—" He gripped his Styrofoam cup. "Mackenzie?"

"Yes?"

"I want to ask you something, and before you laugh or . . . I don't know, slap me, I want you to promise me you'll consider it."

She nodded slowly, obviously having no clue what he was talking about. "All right."

Ben lifted his gaze to meet hers. Her green eyes were wide, her attention totally focused on him. "Mackenzie, will you marry me?"

Eleven

Mackenzie would have sworn she hadn't heard Ben correctly, except that she knew she had. For a moment, she was too stunned to speak. "M . . . marry you?" she managed when she found her voice.

"I know it sounds crazy, but I mean it. I want you to marry me." Ben's words came out in a rush, breathless, without pause. "I really care for you, Mackenzie. I'm in love with you." He met her gaze, his blue eyes searching hers. "And if you would be honest, I think your feelings for me are very strong, too. The minute I met you—this time." He gave her a boyish grin. "I knew you were different than all those other women. I knew you were the woman for me, which is pretty amazing because before that moment, I didn't think there was a woman for me." He met her gaze. "I'm babbling."

She couldn't help chuckling; it eased the tension. "You're babbling."

"I'm sorry. I just wanted to get it all out."

Mackenzie slipped her hands across the table and covered his. They were shaking. His and hers. She didn't know what to say, even where to start. Marry him? The thought was crazy, of course. Ben was babbling all right. He was distracted with worry over his father and obviously didn't know what he was saying.

But a part of her was intrigued by the thought.

"You know," Ben took a deep breath and went on. "Men and women used to be paired off by their parents. Two hundred years ago, you and I might never have met until our wedding day. My father thinks you're perfect for me, and I've made so many bad choices over the years that I'm thinking maybe he knows better than I do." He pulled one hand out from under hers and covered the other. "You've as much as come out and said your choices of men in the past were bad ones. And I know you're lonely. . . ." He exhaled. "As lonely as I am." He took her hands in his and lifted them to his mouth. He kissed her index finger. "Think what fun it would be really getting to know other, knowing we were stuck with each other for the rest of our lives."

She frowned. "Somehow that doesn't sound appealing."

"You know what I mean. With my relationships in the past, there was never any commitment. Not even the thought of a commitment. That meant there was never anything to gain or lose."

Mackenzie listened quietly, making no attempt to question Ben's gibberish. He was crazy with worry and totally exhausted. He didn't know what he was saying.

And yet, in a crazy way, he did make sense. He was right; she was lonely. And she knew that when Nana died, she would be completely alone in the world. At least Ben had good friends nearby; she had left her friends behind with the last move. He was also right when he guessed that she cared a great deal about him. The word *love* had never come into her head, but maybe that was because she had given up a long time ago on the hope of falling in love. Maybe it was because she wasn't even certain what love between a man and a woman was.

Ben grinned, still holding her hands tightly in his. "You will consider it, won't you? You'll consider it because you know what I'm saying makes sense in a whacked-out kind of way."

She couldn't resist a shy smile. "You know, if this is your way of getting me into bed, it's very original. Probably the most original I've ever heard."

He laughed and kissed her fingers again, this time one by one. "We should just do it. We should go downtown and get our license Monday and marry the following Monday. That's all it takes. Just think, in one week we could be married."

By then Max would be out of the woods, Mackenzie thought. Would Ben feel differently then? Not that she was really considering marrying a complete stranger.

Okay, so he wasn't a complete stranger; he was the stranger she'd had a crush on for the last twenty years.

"I think we need to go home and get some sleep," Mackenzie said carefully. "You need to seriously consider your proposal."

"I don't need to consider it. I know what I want and I want you, Mackenzie. I want to make a life with you."

Ben's words were the words Mackenzie had

prayed for, long ago given up on. Did she dare take the chance?

"Well, *I* need to consider your proposal." She rose from the table, somehow feeling differently than she had when she sat down. Suddenly her world seemed so full of hope, of possibilities she'd not even dreamed before. A married woman could have a child. A married woman from a two-income family could work part-time to concentrate on her art. A married woman could climb into bed every night with a man who loved her for who she was, not what she looked like.

"That means you're going to consider it. You're seriously going to consider marrying me, aren't you?" He swept up their cups, tossed them into the trash, and followed her toward the elevator. He was like a kid, almost bouncing with excitement.

"Your buddies will think you're off your rocker. They'll have you committed if you show up to work next Monday a married man."

Ben grabbed her around the waist, and though Mackenzie was normally self-conscious about public displays of affection, she didn't mind this time. There was no one around but a janitor and a volunteer worker wiping down the lunch counter near the cash register.

Ben held her tightly, forcing her to meet his gaze eye to eye. "I love you, Mackenzie, and I want you to marry me. Next Monday," he said firmly.

Ben seemed so sure of himself. He said he loved her. Could that possibly be? Could he barely know her and yet love her? Mackenzie had never believed in love at first sight. She wasn't even certain she believed in romantic love anymore, but Nana had sworn she had fallen for Mackenzie's grandfather the moment she had laid eyes on him. Nana met Pap at their own wedding.

"Will you marry me?" Ben repeated.

Her words tumbled out of her mouth, almost of their own accord. "I'll think about it. It's crazy. It's completely insane, but I'll think about it."

He brought his mouth close to her, his gaze searching hers. "You want to say yes, don't you? For once in your life, you want to do something utterly insane. You want to take a chance." He stroked the corner of her mouth with the pad of his thumb. It was an innocent enough gesture, yet conveyed so much.

Mackenzie felt dizzy. Her heart was pounding so loudly that she could hear it in her head. Her legs were actually weak. Was this what love felt like?

"Marry me, Mackenzie," he cajoled.

Mackenzie didn't know what came over her. The lateness of the hour, maybe. The beer she'd had at the poker game. Maybe the hospital was pumping in some kind of crazy gas into the basement coffee shop, because without considering the seriousness of the word, she whispered, "Yes."

His blue eyes lit up. "Yes? Yes?" he breathed against her mouth.

"Yes," she repeated. "I'll marry you, Ben."

He brought his mouth to hers in the sweetest, most romantic kiss and Mackenzie melted in his arms. Their tongues met, entwined. He tasted of coffee and promise.

It was Mackenzie who pulled away first, breathless, still dizzy. Excited, happy beyond words. "We should go home," she whispered.

"Yeah, because if we don't go home now," he

murmured in her ear, his voice husky, "I'm not sure I'll be able to keep my hands off you." He kissed her lobe. "And I think we ought to save that for our wedding night, don't you."

Our wedding night. His words rang in Mackenzie's ears and she felt her skin flush.

Ben grinned ear to ear as he ran his hand across her back. "I'll walk you to your car."

"Okay," she breathed, still a little unsteady on her feet.

Outside, in the cold, dark parking lot, Ben unlocked her car and let her in. He closed the door and she put down the window.

"Sleep in tomorrow, and I'll call you."

"Church," she said.

"What?"

"Church. I'll go to church in the morning, then stop by to see Nana. I'll meet you here around eleven. You'll be here, right?"

"Yeah, yeah, right." He leaned in the window and kissed her. This time his kiss was chaste, almost husbandlike.

It sent a thrill down her spine just the same.

" 'Night."

" 'Night."

Mackenzie put up the window and pulled out of the parking spot. As she turned onto the lighted street, she glanced in her rearview mirror.

Ben, bless his heart, was standing there in the cold, waving.

It had been a long time since someone had waved to her as she pulled away. Too long.

* * *

The following morning, Mackenzie swept into her grandmother's room at the nursing home. "Nana! How are you this morning?"

Mackenzie had gone right to bed, slept soundly the remainder of the night, and woke filled with a strange sense of excitement and wonder. For a moment she had questioned if she had dreamed Ben's proposal to her, but the reality of the bright sunshine pouring in her bedroom window made her realize it was true. Unless she got cold feet or a train hit one of them, she would be Ben's wife one week from tomorrow.

"I brought you a church bulletin," Mackenzie said, approaching the side of the bed to kiss her grandmother good morning. "I know you like to hear what songs we sang and what liturgy we recited."

Nana laid in her hospital bed, her arms at her side, staring at the wall in front of her. She'd already been bathed this morning and was wearing a flowered housecoat over her hospital gown. Her thin hair was still damp around her ears.

Mackenzie sat on the edge of the chair beside her grandmother's bed and stared at the old woman's face. "Oh, Nana, I wish I could tell if you can understand me," she said wistfully.

She paused and then continued. "I have exciting news to tell you. Well, at least I hope you'll think it's exciting news."

She took a deep breath and slipped her hand over her grandmother's. "I'm getting married," Mackenzie whispered excitedly. "Next week."

Nana didn't blink.

"I know this is sudden, but believe it or not, I've

known him twenty years. It's Ben Gordon. I went to high school with him." She gave a little laugh. "He was the boy I asked to the senior prom and he turned me down. Remember? I wanted to quit school and become a missionary in South America. You made me go to the prom with your friend Frieda's son, Oscar."

Mackenzie watched her grandmother's face for any sign of comprehension. Nothing.

"We're getting our license and blood tests tomorrow. Getting married next Monday. Just a civil ceremony. I know you won't like that idea, but we're very busy, me with work and the Tree Festival, and Ben with his business." She squeezed her grandmother's hand. "I want you to be happy for me, because I'm happy."

Mackenzie detected the strangest sensation beneath her hand. *Movement*. Nana had moved her hand in Mackenzie's!

Mackenzie's first reaction was to assume it was her imagination, or just a muscle spasm, but when she met Nana's gaze, she knew better. Not a muscle had moved on her grandmother's face, but something about her eyes was different . . . almost a twinkle. It only lasted a moment, and then the blank stare was there again, but Mackenzie was certain she hadn't been mistaken.

Mackenzie felt the tears trickle down her face as she squeezed her grandmother's hand back. "You do hear me, don't you? You hear every word I say to you," she said excitedly. "You've understood everything I've said since the day you moved in here. Oh, Nana, I'm so happy." She leaned over and kissed the old woman's papery cheek. She smelled of lavender bath powder. "You're trying to tell me you approve, aren't you?" She sniffed back her tears. "I'm so glad you approve."

Mackenzie pulled back to look into her grandmother's eyes again. "I'll bring him in to meet you, okay? I'll bring him in before we get married." Wiping her tears from her cheeks, she settled down in the chair again.

"His father's had a heart attack and he's in the hospital, so this week will be hectic, but I promise I'll bring him by." She reached for the newspaper on the table beside the bed, where she'd dropped it when she came in the room. "So what will it be first? I know you like the obituaries and the births. That or the funnies?" She flipped through the pages. "Okay, funnies it is."

After a short visit with her grandmother, Mackenie drove to the hospital. As she rode the elevator up to the second floor, she actually felt nervous about seeing Ben. What if he had changed his mind? Better now than a week and a day from now, she knew, but now that she had decided to take this crazy chance, she desperately wanted to take it all the way.

Mackenzie swung her purse over her shoulder and knocked on the open hospital room door.

Ben rose from the chair beside his father's bed. "Morning."

She felt shy and awkward in the doorway. After all these years, she was comfortable with her height, but in the pumps she'd worn to church, she was actually a hair taller than Ben. She wondered if she should have changed.

Ben slipped his hand around her waist and kissed her cheek. "How are you?"

She smiled. "Good." She turned to Max who was sitting up in bed flipping the channels on the TV from a remote control in his hand. "How are you, Mr. Gordon?"

Max glanced at her. "Mr. Gordon, who the hell is that? Call me Max. Everyone I give two fleas for does." He changed the channel again. "Anyone that calls me Mr. Gordon around here is taking my blood or shooting something in my butt."

Mackenzie met Ben's gaze, trying not to laugh.

"Dad's a little edgy this morning."

"Wouldn't give me my prune juice," Max muttered. "Had to send Ben downstairs to the cafeteria for some."

Mackenzie nodded, realizing Max didn't really expect her to comment, just listen.

"Hey," Ben said quietly from beside her. "Can I talk to you for a minute." He glanced into the hallway, meaning he wanted to talk in private.

Oh, no. He'd changed his mind. The light of day had made him realize what a ridiculous idea it was for them to marry, and he was going to tell her so.

Mackenzie swallowed hard, clutching her purse. She was being silly. Overreacting. Even if he did want to break off the engagement that was less than twelve hours old, it was his right, wasn't it? And she certainly didn't want to marry someone who didn't want to marry her.

They stepped out into the hall. A nurse in a

bright-green smock and carrying a tray passed them. Ben waited for her to go by.

"Um, last night we didn't really discuss who we were going to tell—"

Mackenzie knew Ben heard her let out a sigh of relief.

He caught her hand in his. "You know, about us getting married. What did you think I wanted to talk to you about?"

She shook her head. "Never mind. Listen, we're going to have to tell people eventually."

He laughed. "I know, but I was thinking that maybe we should just keep this to ourselves, because well, you know people are going to try and talk us out of it."

"You mean Zack and Owen."

He hemmed. "Yeah, maybe. It is kind of sudden."

She shrugged. Truthfully, she didn't have anyone to tell. "That's fine, whatever you think's best." She glanced past him at his father in the hospital bed. "Although I really think you ought to tell your dad."

Ben pressed his broad hand to the small of her back. "You're right. I thought we would tell Dad. It might speed up his recovery. Last night when I came in to see him, he was really worked up about me being alone."

Mackenzie watched Ben carefully for any signs that he might be having second thoughts. She didn't detect any. "And you're sure we should just go ahead and do this? Not wait?"

"Zack said that not waiting was the best decision he and Kayla made."

Mackenzie laughed. "But they had gone on more than two dates, hadn't they?"

Ben laughed with her and then leaned forward to kiss her lips. "I think we need to just go for it, Mackenzie. We just have to trust ourselves and how we feel about each other."

"Okay," she said nodding, still relieved. "We'll just go for it." She glanced through Max's doorway again. "So what's going on with your dad?"

"More testing and an angioplasty tomorrow or Tuesday."

"So do we make plans to meet at the courthouse to apply for the marriage license or what?"

"First thing in the morning," he said firmly. "I'll meet you, take care of that, and then come over here. What do you have going tomorrow?"

She felt so giddy inside that it was strange to be having such a normal conversation with him. "I've got that barn of a house to finish up—maybe by the end of the week if I get a move on."

He leaned toward her again, this time touching her nose with the tip of his. "Oh, I don't know, the customer might cut you some slack, for certain favors," he said, his voice low and sexy.

"Oh, no. I'm finishing that job before I move in." She looked at him quickly. "If that's what you want me to do, of course."

"Well, I do intend to live with you, and moving into my place makes more sense than moving into yours," he teased. "And then there's Dad. That's going to be all right isn't it?"

"Of course! Well . . . as long as I can bring Howard. I'm not going anywhere without Howard."

"We're going to make quite a family, aren't we?" Ben laughed with her.

"Hey, what are you two doing out there? What are you laughing about?" Max hollered. "If anyone's going to be telling jokes, I think I ought to be in on it. I'm the one sitting here in this bed with a hundred and twenty-one channels and nothing to watch."

Ben grabbed Mackenzie's hand and led her into the hospital room again. "Okay, Dad." He glanced at Mackenzie, so excited he looked as if he might burst. "Wait until you hear this one. . . ."

Twelve

For the umpteenth time, Ben glanced at the small retro-style clock on his desk in his office. The hands seemed to be moving incredibly slowly. Mackenzie said she was stopping to see her grandmother, going by the market, and then she'd be home. Another five minutes and he could call her.

In the meantime, he had some invoices that needed his attention. He'd spent so much time at the hospital with his dad this week that he had fallen behind with work. Bills needed to be paid and sent. If he didn't bill clients, Land's End Renovations didn't get paid and subsequently neither did he, Zack, or Owen. In the past, Ben had never thought much about money; he'd always lived comfortably on his salary. But thinking about the fact that he would be a married man in three days gave him a certain sense of responsibility he'd never possessed before. He and Mackenzie would be husband and wife in a few days and they would be responsible for each other. A short time ago, that responsibility would have scared the wits out of him, but as he typed information into his computer and printed out bills, he found he kind of liked it.

Three days, he thought. Three days and he would

be married. Max had practically leaped out of his hospital bed with excitement at the news. He had thrown his arms around Mackenzie and hugged her as if she were already his daughter-in-law. Seeing his father so pleased had pleased Ben. His father's reaction was proof to him that he was making the right decision in marrying Mackenzie without delay.

The angioplasty on Wednesday had gone well for Max, and he was scheduled to be released tomorrow morning. Mackenzie was close to finishing painting the living room; all she needed to do now was replace the painted receptacles and unstick the windows. While she worked, Ben would get Max settled at home; then they would start moving Mackenzie's belongings over to the house. Ben thought it would be a fun way to spend the afternoon. This way, they could get something accomplished, while still keeping an eye on Max, without his knowing it. His physicians were expecting a complete recovery, but Ben still wanted to stay close to home, at least for a few days.

Ben glanced at the clock. Mackenzie should have arrived at home by now. He dialed her and she picked up right away.

"Hi, Ben."

He rocked back in his chair, grinning. Smitten. He was definitely smitten. He had never known he was capable of these feelings for a woman. "How did you know it was me?"

"Because you said you would call and because no one else ever calls me."

He could tell by the sound of her voice that she was smiling, too.

He fingered the glossy pamphlet for a hotel lying

on his desk blotter. He had picked it up at the travel agency in town in the "local" section. "I made arrangements for Monday night. Want to hear about it?"

"Nah." Her voice was sexy. "Surprise me."

Ben had made a reservation for one night at a hotel over in Ocean City, Maryland. It was right between the bay and the ocean, and was perfect for a one-night honeymoon, or so the receptionist had promised him. Despite the snow on the ground and the gray of early December, Ben thought it would be romantic to sit in the living room curled up on the couch beside the fireplace and gaze out over the water. He hoped Mackenzie would think so, too.

"What about Max? Are you sure we should leave him?" He could hear Howie chuffing and Mackenzie making noise as she banged around in her kitchen. "Because I really don't mind postponing the honeymoon," she continued. "We could wait a few months, until things are less hectic, and then go somewhere for a whole week. Maybe in the spring."

"I fully intend to take my wife away for a honeymoon for a whole week," Ben assured her. He liked the way "my wife" sounded when he said it aloud. "But I still think we should do this now. It's just one night."

"I really need to get your living room finished and then do something about hiring a new crew," she said.

"*Our* living room in three days," he corrected.

"Our living room."

"Come on, Mackenzie, you're making excuses."

He lowered his voice. "That isn't like you. Don't you want to go away for the night with me?"

"You bet I do, Ben Gordon." The laughter that came over the phone was sultry and full of promise. "I just don't want you to think I'm insensitive about your father."

"I don't think you're being insensitive and the reservation has been made. Everything has been arranged. Kayla is going to keep an eye on Dad, and should she think it's necessary, she'll spend Monday night here with him."

"You told her?" she asked incredulously.

He studied the hotel pamphlet with its photo of a Jacuzzi bathtub overlooking the bay and a fireplace flickering in the background. He couldn't stop thinking about being alone with Mackenzie in the hotel room, alone and married to her. He couldn't stop thinking about making love to her. "No, I didn't tell her. We agreed we wouldn't tell anyone but Dad and your grandmother until after we get home Tuesday. I just told her I needed to take care of some personal business."

"Personal business, eh?"

Again, that throaty laughter. Just hearing her voice made Ben feel strangely warm. Sure, he found her sexually arousing, but there was something more to Mackenzie Sayer. Something amazing.

"So, did you call for a reason?" Mackenzie asked.

"Just to hear your voice."

"Now you're overdoing it, buster."

He chuckled. "Hey! I worked on the trees today."

"You did? Oh, Ben, I told you not to worry about the Christmas trees. I could have figured something out. With your dad sick and—"

"Never let it be said that Ben Gordon doesn't come through on his promises. I'll be there with all the other sponsors decorating my trees on Wednesday night."

"So are you going to tell me what your themes are?" She sounded intrigued, and he liked the idea of being mysterious to her.

"Nope. You'll have to wait and see."

"Well, I've got to work on my ornaments, so I'd better go."

Mackenzie had shown Ben a box of wooden birds she had carved for her Christmas tree. They were strikingly beautiful, crude in one way and yet so realistic in another that when Ben had touched a sparrow he had almost thought that he felt its heartbeat through its feathered chest. She had explained that the style was considered folk art. He'd been very impressed by her wildlife-by-the-bay paintings, but even more impressed by the carvings. He intended to bid and win her tree if it took every penny of his life savings. He couldn't imagine a better way to celebrate their first Christmas together than around a tree decorated by Mackenzie's hand.

A moment of silence hung between them. Ben had to go, too. He wanted to call the hospital and say good night to his dad, and he still had work to do. Just the same, he wasn't ready to hang up. He was about to embark on the adventure of his life with this woman and right now, he didn't want to let go of her, not even for a second. "I miss you," he said.

"You can't miss me," she teased, obviously pleased. "You saw me less than an hour and a half ago."

He tucked one hand behind his head. He still couldn't believe that he was going to be married by this time Monday. Him, the founding father of Bachelors Inc. "Call me before you go to bed?"

"You bet."

"How's it going?" Ben walked up behind Mackenzie and kissed the top of her head.

His innocent display of affection seemed very husbandly and pleased her. This was going to work. It really was going to work.

Mackenzie was on her knees replacing the last electrical receptacle her crew had painted over. "I'm just about done here." She came to her feet, brandishing a power screwdriver. She was dressed in her paint coveralls and a ball cap. Just being close to Ben made her feel warm all over and just a little unsettled. She wondered how long it would take once they were married for this feeling to go away. She wondered if it ever would.

All week Mackenzie had purposefully not thought much about the impulsive decision to marry Ben. Instead, she kept herself focused on everything she had to get done and on the actual idea of being married to him. If her grandmother and grandfather could make it work, she and Ben could make it work. It was that simple. They were in love, at least in the beginning stages of love, and as Max had pointed out in his hospital room the night they gave him their news, sometimes people just have to take chances.

Mackenzie smoothed the pocket of Ben's faded blue oxford shirt. "How's Max?"

He shrugged. "Says he's fine. He didn't even want to lie down when he got home from the hospital. I practically had to wrestle him into the bed. He's already asleep now, so he must have needed the nap. I'm sure all of that rigmarole he had to go through this morning to get checked out tired him. But his cardiologist said that other than taking it easy for a few days and getting plenty of fluids and rest, he can go back to his daily routine."

She carried the battery-powered screwdriver to her toolbox and dropped it in. "What about exercise? Can he go back to swimming laps at the senior center?"

"Well, he has a checkup next week. He's supposed to lay low until then, but the doctor seemed pretty confident he could start swimming again after that."

She smiled. "The wonders of modern medical technology are amazing. I'm so glad he's going to be okay."

"He gave me quite a scare." Ben hooked his thumbs into his jean pockets. "But, you know, if he hadn't scared me, I don't know that I would have had the nerve to ask you to marry me." He grabbed her by the hips and pulled her against him. "So for that I'm truly thankful."

Mackenzie molded her body to Ben's and turned her head slightly to meet his lips. One kiss, and her veins were pulsing, her heart pounding. Something about the forbidden made her want him all the more. She couldn't wait until their wedding Monday. No, she couldn't wait until Monday night when they consummated the marriage. Almost forty years old and she was feeling like a virgin again. It scared her and delighted her at the same time.

Ben moaned softly as she stroked his back. She could feel his groin hardening against hers.

"Are you sure we couldn't have a little prenuptial—"

"Absolutely not." She pulled back, but not out of his arms.

He grinned. "You can't blame a man for asking. Not when his fiancée is such a hot box lunch."

"A hot box lunch?" She lifted an eyebrow. "I take it that's good?"

"Definitely good," he said in a deep, sexy voice. He brought his lips to hers, pulling her tighter.

"Afternoon."

"Hey, guys."

Mackenzie turned her head to see Zack and Owen walking into the living room. They were carrying white bags from the deli and the aroma of corned beef wafted from them.

"Don't you guys knock?" Ben demanded, releasing her from his embrace.

"Nope," Zack said.

"You don't," Owen answered. "Hey, Mackenzie."

"Hi, Mackenzie," Zack followed.

Mackenzie could see it was going to take some time to get used to Ben's friends. Over the years, she'd certainly had friends, but not like these guys were friends. She wasn't the jealous type, but a part of her envied Ben and Zack and Owen, and even Abby. They had known Ben for so long, knew so much about him, and she knew so little.

But she was marrying him on Monday.

"We brought lunch," Owen said, walking into the kitchen behind Zack.

Mackenzie and Ben had no choice but to follow them.

"And to what do we owe the honor of this visit?" Ben asked suspiciously.

"No reason." Zack helped himself to glasses in the cupboard. "Just came by to see how Max is."

"Max is fine." Ben stood in the doorway. "And you knew that because I already talked to both of you this morning."

"Well, we're glad he's doing well. We were worried." Owen began doling out sandwiches at the kitchen table.

Ben eyed Mackenzie and then gestured toward the table. "Lunch?"

She shrugged. "Lunch it is."

Zack, Mackenzie, and Ben took their seats and Owen brought everyone a Coke.

Owen sat down, took one bite of his sandwich and then set it down. "So, kids." He clapped his hands, looking to Ben and Mackenzie. "Any news?"

Mackenzie almost choked on her corned beef. She met Ben's gaze across the table. He never flinched, although she saw a flicker of surprise in his eyes before he reached for a handful of potato chips, as if he didn't have a care in the world. "News?" He shook his head, playing it cool. "No news here. You, Mackenzie?"

She followed his lead, grabbing potato chips. She didn't even like potato chips. "No news here. Except that my garbage disposal is broken at the apartment. Anyone know how to fix a garbage disposal that's eaten a spoon?"

Ben flashed her a grin that made her relax a little. Yes, these men were Ben's best friends, but she and Ben were partners now. That was what he was telling her. Partners in crime, at the moment.

"No news at all. Fancy that." Zack took a drink of the cola and made a face. "I don't know how you guys drink this stuff." He pushed his glass away and got up from his chair. "Got any juice?"

Ben rocked back in his chair. "In the fridge."

"No news at all," Owen repeated. "Huh."

"What, are you guys working up some kind of comedy routine?" Ben asked. "Because so far, it's not going very well."

Mackenzie chuckled and took another bite of her sandwich. She enjoyed the wordplay between the three men. She enjoyed watching their camaraderie.

"So nothing's happening here, say . . . on *Monday*?" Zack said.

Mackenzie stiffened, but she continued eating as if nothing were amiss. She understood if Ben didn't want to tell his friends until after he was married. He said it was because he didn't want to argue with them. It occurred to her that maybe he was afraid they might be able to convince him to change his mind, but she pushed that thought away. Ben's mind was already made up.

"Oh! Monday!" Ben reached for more chips. "You're talking about Monday."

Mackenzie lowered her gaze to her sandwich to keep from looking at Ben. Was he going to tell them?

"Yeah, Monday." Zack sat down with a glass of orange juice.

"Monday I'm going away overnight. I've got something to take care of over in Ocean City. I'll be home Tuesday."

"Something to take care of," Owen repeated.

"Didn't Kayla tell you?" Ben asked Zack. "She's going to keep an eye on Dad for me."

"She did tell me. Actually she didn't tell me anything other than that she was keeping an eye on Max." Zack looked to Owen. "That's what has us worried. I mean, you wouldn't do anything crazy would you? Not without telling us."

"What are you talking about? Of course I wouldn't." Ben got up. "Mackenzie, want more Coke?"

She shook her head, afraid to speak.

"Well, we're glad to hear that, Ben," Owen said. "We just wouldn't want you making any impulsive decisions, not with the stress you're under right now with the business and your dad being sick and all."

"No crazy decisions here," Ben repeated coming back to the table. "So how about them Redskins. . . ."

It was a full hour before Zack and Owen finally left and Mackenzie could be alone with Ben. He closed the door behind them, and she threw herself into his arms. "Oh, my gosh. They know!"

He rubbed her shoulder. "They don't know."

She rolled her eyes. "Okay, they don't know, but obviously they suspect something."

"Let them suspect." He grabbed her hand and

led her out of the mudroom into the living room. "By Tuesday they'll know the truth."

She halted in the middle of the living room and searched his gaze. "And you're okay with that?"

He kissed her lightly on the lips. "It's what I want, Mackenzie. I want this to be between just the two of us. Our decision. I don't need their input to know that I'm in love with you and that, more importantly, I want to spend the rest of my life with you as your husband."

He said the word *husband* loudly, firmly, as if he meant it, and his conviction sent her fears skittering under the rug again. "I do love you," she said quietly, still testing the sound of the words. She'd said it before, but it had never felt like this.

"I love you," he whispered. "Now let's check on Dad and get over to your place with those empty boxes. I want all but your killer bod officially moved in by tomorrow night."

She grinned. "That's right. The bod is not officially yours until Monday."

He grabbed her around the waist and kissed her again. "And for that, I can't wait."

Thirteen

"That's it?" Mackenzie whispered against Ben's lips, her heart pounding as she stood in the center of the small room at the Land's End courthouse staring at Ben, a bouquet of white winter rosebuds clutched in her sweaty palms.

"That's it." Ben grinned. "You heard the justice of the peace pronounce us man and wife."

Man and wife. *Married.*

Since the morning of the blood tests, she had known this was what they were moving toward. Yet, as she stood here in the quiet, simple room with its ivory-white walls and pale-blue carpet, she realized that she was a man's wife. She was Ben Gordon's wife. *Until death did they part.*

Mackenzie swallowed hard, stifling the tightening sense of panic she felt in the pit of her stomach. Ben certainly didn't look panicked; in fact, he looked quite pleased with himself.

"Here you go," said the justice of the peace, an attractive, plump woman in her early sixties. "Your marriage certificate."

Ben reached for the white envelope. "That's it, Jane?"

She smiled as if she herself had arranged their

meeting, courtship, and nuptials. "That's it. Congratulations." She shook both of their hands.

Mackenzie smiled woodenly. It wasn't that she was having second thoughts. She just felt numb. She hadn't realized how such a short, simple ceremony could have such a deep impact on the rest of someone's life. On two lives.

"Now, remember you promised you wouldn't say anything," Ben told Jane. "We want to surprise everyone tomorrow after we get back from Ocean City."

"Bennett! I'm shocked you would say such a thing. I'm a court official of the state of Maryland. Whatever takes place behind these doors is confidential." Her dark eyes twinkled. "But they're going to be surprised, all right. Up until a few minutes ago, you were considered the most sought-after bachelor in Land's End."

Ben chuckled as he reached out for Jane's hand again and then, instead, wrapped his arms around her and gave her a big bear hug. "Thanks, dear. I knew we could count on you."

Jane laughed, flustered and delighted at the same time by Ben's attention. Every female liked this man, from infants to centenarians.

Ben turned to the man and woman standing behind them. One was a clerk in Jane's office, the other a town cop. "Thanks so much for witnessing for us, Cassie and John." Ben shook one's hand and then the other.

"Just so you don't tell Zack and Owen it was us," Cassie, the cop said. "You know they'd be bent out of shape that we were here and they weren't invited."

Mackenzie offered her hand to the two witnesses whom she had never seen in her life before she walked into the little brick courthouse at noon. She murmured her thank-yous, and she and Ben were in their coats and out of the building a minute later.

Just outside the doors, at the top of the steps, Ben surprised Mackenzie by throwing his arms around her. "I'm so happy," he murmured, snuggling his face between the collar of her black, wool coat and her gray scarf.

She hugged him back, still feeling a little unsteady of mind and body. "Me, too."

"Yeah?" He met her gaze, his blue eyes shockingly bright on the cold day.

"Yeah." She leaned forward, kissed him, and then grabbed his hand. "But I'm also cold. Can we get in the car?"

Laughing, they ran hand in hand down the steps, avoiding patches of ice, and into the parking lot. Inside Ben's Explorer, they cranked up the heat and waited for the warmth to shoot out of the vents.

"Fogging up in here," Mackenzie said, redirecting her vent.

"Perfect opportunity."

She turned her head. "For what?"

"This." Ben leaned between the two seats and brushed his lips against hers. "How long is this ride over to Ocean City?" he murmured against her mouth.

The kiss was delicious, warm and full of a sense of excitement to come.

"It was your idea to go all the way to Ocean

City." She flicked her tongue over his lower lip. "I'd have settled for my apartment."

He slid his arm around her shoulder, pulling her toward him, off the seat. "There's no furniture left in your apartment. Besides, that's not romantic enough." He stroked beneath her chin with the pad of his thumb, his voice low and sexy. "I want our first time to be romantic."

Our first time. Mackenzie had thought of little else for the last twenty-four hours. She wanted to make love to Ben; she only hoped she would satisfy him. She knew he'd probably been with a lot of women in the past and— Mackenzie forced her insecurities out of her head. She was Ben's wife now, she told herself. Of course she could satisfy him.

Ben kissed Mackenzie again and gazed into her eyes. "Ready to go?"

She laughed, her own voice husky with desire for him. "I think we'd better, else we're liable to consummate right here in the parking lot."

He laughed with her as he sat up, put on his seat belt and slid the car into reverse. "That probably wouldn't be wise, not with Cassie still in the courthouse."

"I think you're right." Mackenzie giggled at the thought of the policewoman entering the parking lot to find a newly married couple *consummating* in the parking lot. "She'd have to arrest us for indecent exposure or something."

Ben and Mackenzie laughed again and their laughter eased them into conversation. They drove east along little country roads and eventually picked up Route 404 to the Delaware/Maryland beaches.

At an intersection on Delaware's main highway, Ben stopped for a red light.

"I need a kiss," he stated.

"Another?" She slid over in her seat toward him, all too happy to oblige. The Explorer was toasty warm now and they had both taken off their coats. Mackenzie had worn off-white wool pants and a cream-colored lambswool sweater. They had both agreed they would dress casually for the wedding. After all, it wasn't about what they wore or where it took place, but about how they felt about each other. Ben was wearing gray, wool dress pants and a black sweater with a mock turtleneck. Very sexy.

Mackenzie met his lips. "Aren't we there yet?"

He eased his tongue between her lips, and she tasted the coffee they had shared a short time ago. The car smelled of warm wool, vanilla almond coffee, and their desire for each other.

"We could stop at a hotel once we hit the coast," he suggested. His breath in her ear made her skin tingle.

"That would be silly. Frivolous." She lifted her lashes to meet his gaze. "Wouldn't it?"

A car honked its horn behind them. The light had turned green.

Ben flashed her a charmingly boyish grin. "It would be." He pulled across the intersection and hit the gas.

Mackenzie slipped her arm around Ben, cuddling against him as best she could while still remaining in her seatbelt. "So how close is the nearest cheap motel?"

"Give me half an hour, lady."

* * *

By the time Ben got the key from the front desk and he and Mackenzie took the elevator up to their "clean but affordable" room, she was trembling all over. They had kissed on the bottom floor and then again at the top. Ben had hit the CLOSE DOOR button three times to give them a little privacy.

They were both laughing, sliding their hands beneath each other's coats as they stumbled toward their room at the end of the hall. At Room 210 Ben eased Mackenzie against the wall that was carpeted halfway to the ceiling and she slipped her arms around his neck. She parted her lips and tasted his tongue, pulling him closer, molding her body to his.

Breathless, panting, Ben fumbled with the card key in the door while she pressed soft kisses to his neck.

Ben muttered something in frustration.

Mackenzie peered at the door as he shoved the key in again.

The light blinked red.

"Try again," she said.

He was laughing, but his voice was husky. She knew he wanted her as much as she wanted him right now.

Again, the light blinked red and the doorknob wouldn't turn.

"Let me try." She was so nervous, so excited, that she was getting giggly. She slid the card into the slot as he wrapped his arms around her from behind.

Red again.

"It doesn't work," she said in frustration, turning to him.

He pushed her against the door. "What do you mean it doesn't work?" He kissed her between words.

"It doesn't work!" She pushed the key into his hand. "Go get another. The clerk didn't program it correctly."

He looked down the long hall, running a hand through his hair that was no longer neatly combed. She must have done that in the elevator.

"I have to go back?"

"I'll wait here." She could feel her heart thudding in her chest, and her breath was a little short as if they had taken the stairs instead of the elevator.

"You don't want to ride the elevator with me?" he asked in his voice that now seemed to be perpetually husky.

She grinned back. "I don't think that's safe at this point, do you?"

He kissed her again and hurried down the hall, his long, black, wool coat flapping behind him. "I'll be right back." He waved the useless key. "Don't go anywhere!"

She leaned against the door, thankful the hall was deserted at two in the afternoon. "Where would I go?"

Ben disappeared in the elevator and Mackenzie waited at the door. She wrapped her arms around her waist, hugging herself. Ben wasn't just sexy and smart, he was fun, too. She'd never really had fun with men before, not like this. Not about sex. She had never known she really liked fun. But she did.

It seemed as if an eternity passed before the elevator finally dinged and Ben shot out into the hall.

Mackenzie couldn't help laughing. She felt silly and exhilarated at the same time. How could two adults their age—a husband and wife, no less—be so desperate to have sex?

"If this doesn't work," Ben said, pushing his coat back as if he were Superman, "I'm breaking down the door!"

Luckily for hotel maintenance, the door opened on the first try.

"Green light, go!" Ben pushed open the door, grabbed her hand, and pulled her inside.

Mackenzie fell against the door, closing it. She saw the key card slide from Ben's hand as he pulled off her coat. She yanked off his, letting it fall to the floor on top of hers. They embraced, mouth-to-mouth, limb-to-limb. Trills of excitement pulsed through her veins as they kissed.

Ben slid his hand upward over her hip, up her rib cage under her breast over the wool of her sweater. She sucked in her breath as his hand met with the curve of her flesh. One stroke and she wanted more, had to have more.

Mackenzie reached for the hem of her sweater and yanked it over her head. Her hair and sweater crackled with static electricity that seemed to arc between them. Ben took the sweater from her hand and added it to the growing pile of discarded clothing.

She was wearing an ivory lace bra. The panties matched, but she doubted he would notice. At this point, she wondered why she had taken such care in choosing her undergarments this morning. It was actually kind of funny.

Still leaning against the door, Mackenzie pressed

her palms to the paneled wood as he lowered his face between her breasts that thrust from above the underwire and lace bra. A shiver of pleasure went through her. She had had sex before and couldn't say she hadn't enjoyed it, but this was so different, so spontaneous and urgent. In the past, she always felt self-conscious about how she looked, how she sounded, even how she smelled. None of that mattered now, only Ben and his hands and his mouth on her.

He reached behind her and unhooked her bra on the first try. She refused to dwell on how many times he had done that for other women. None of them mattered now, just her. Mackenzie Gordon, his wife.

Ben cupped her full breasts in his hands and lifted them to his mouth. Mackenzie let her eyes drift shut as she moaned with pleasure. He caught one nipple between his lips and her legs trembled. She gripped his shoulder for support as he made tiny sucking motions with his mouth. She was burning up and his wool sweater was hot and rough where it brushed her skin.

She grabbed the hem of his sweater and pulled it over his head. His chest was broad and muscular, his biceps and triceps well defined. She had seen the weight-lifting equipment in his spare room, but was pleasantly surprised to see that he actually used it.

The hard flesh of his chest met with the soft roundness of her breasts and his crisp chest hair tickled delightfully.

They embraced again, kissing, stroking. She loved the feel of his hard muscles under her fingers.

"Want to go to the bed?" he murmured. "More comfortable?"

"Probably be smart." She gave a little laugh, resting a hand on his shoulder as she balanced on first one foot and then the other to slip off her heeled loafers. "Before I fall over."

Ben kicked out of his own shoes and reached out to take her in his arms.

"What are you doing?" She laughed as he lifted her by the shoulders and beneath her knees, raising her off the floor.

"What do you think I'm doing? You're my wife. This is the first time we're going to make love." He carried her toward the bed. "I want this to be right; I want it to be perfect."

Mackenzie worried that she was too heavy for him. She had never had a man pick her up before. She was as tall as he was, but his gesture was so sweet and so romantic that she relaxed in his arms. He made her feel tiny, treasured.

As he eased her gently onto the coverlet on the bed, her head on the pillow, she looped her arms around his neck. "Thank you," she whispered, surprised by the tears that welled in her eyes.

"For what?"

"For loving me like this."

He kissed her gently this time, not so much with passion but caring. Then he gazed into her eyes. "I love you, Mackenzie. I mean it."

"I love you," she whispered, reaching for the waistband of her pants and wriggling over. "Now get those off and get in here!"

Ben slipped out of his wool pants and socks and helped her pull back the coverlet so that they lay side by side on the clean white sheets. Nothing was between them now but the cotton of his paisley boxers and the silk of her ivory panties.

This time their kiss was less hurried. Their strokes were less frenzied. Ben caressed every inch of her body, exploring, observing her every response. He seemed fascinated not just with the obvious parts of her body, but every crook, every valley, every length of muscle and flesh. He kissed, he stroked, he teased until she was a bundle of aching nervous energy.

"Ben," Mackenzie murmured in his ear. "Make love to me."

"I am," he teased, brushing his lips across her cheek.

"You know what I mean," she breathed.

Ben's fingers rested on the band of her white panties, burning hot where they touched. She lifted her hips against his hand.

"You're teasing," she whispered, afraid to open her eyes, afraid this was all too good to be true. "You know what I want."

He had slipped out of his boxers so when he pressed closer, she could feel the hardness of his desire for her against her bare thigh. "What?" he whispered. "Tell me, Mackenzie."

"You." It came out breathy and low. "I want you, Ben."

He slid her panties down her legs, and she sighed each time his fingers brushed her quivering flesh. Then he raised up on the bed and laid down again, over her, cradling her in his arms.

Mackenzie raised her hands over her head, her hair strewn wild across the pillow and on the sheets.

It was only natural that when she felt the pressure between her thighs, she parted them.

"Mackenzie. . . ." He whispered her name as if it were a song.

She was certainly physically prepared and aching for him, yet nothing had prepared her for the most overwhelming rush of emotion she had ever experienced as he entered her.

Mackenzie arched her back to meet his stroke and closed her eyes against the tears threatening to spill. Ben nestled his face in the crook of her neck and planted soft, fleeting kisses over her hot skin.

He lifted and thrust. She raised her hips to meet him. Every muscle in her body was taut, stretched to the breaking point.

Slowly Ben found a rhythm and together they moved as one. He whispered her name and poignant endearments, all the while pushing her closer and closer toward the edge.

Mackenzie could hear Ben's breathing change. He strained; she arched up against him. A part of her wanted to hold back, to make this sweet aching last forever, but it was impossible.

She sank her fingernails into his back and cried out his name. In one instant, her pleasure and release surged through her body. Inside her head, lights flashed and she heard herself cry out.

He called her name once more and thrust toward his own release. And then it was over, at least for the moment.

Panting, Ben slid off her onto the bed to relieve her of his weight. But he kept an arm wrapped around her and pulled her close, covering her with the corner of the sheet.

Mackenzie snuggled close, a shy smile on her face. She was still afraid to open her eyes.

"Wow," he whispered.

She giggled. "Wow."

Fourteen

Ben pressed a kiss to her damp forehead, and she snuggled against him, enjoying the smell of his hair and the feel of his muscular body against hers beneath the sheet.

She pushed up on one elbow to gaze into his eyes, a silly smile on her face. "I guess that was worth stopping for, huh?"

"Definitely worth stopping for." He grinned as he leaned toward her and kissed her mouth.

She wrinkled her nose. "Do we have to actually check out face-to-face with a clerk or can we leave the key and run?"

He laughed, brushing a lock of blond hair off her cheek. It was a gentle, intimate gesture, one she imagined would take place between a husband and a wife. That simple touch made their lovemaking seem even more magical.

"I paid with my credit card," he told her. "All we have to do is leave the key on the table and sneak out through the back. They'll never know we only needed the room for an hour."

She giggled and lay back on the pillow. "I can't believe we did this, Ben."

"What? Make love? It's what newlyweds do."

She felt her cheeks grow warm, but she wasn't embarrassed. What had been between them here in this bed had been right and good. The best, and she had a ring of gold around her finger that made it even better. "No, silly." She tapped his forearm beneath the sheet. "I meant I can't believe we got married. We've got to be out of our minds!" She turned to gaze into his blue eyes that seemed as deep as the ocean. "We don't even know each other."

"I know you," he said quietly, full of confidence. "I know you're smart and funny and fun to be with." He traced her lips with his forefinger. "And very beautiful and very sensual."

Mackenzie felt as if she were melting beneath the sheet. No one had ever said things like this to her before. Ben was so romantic, so sweet and charming. She couldn't help wondering how she had missed such traits when she'd been only sixteen. So what if he had been a schmuck sometimes then, too? This was the real Ben, the mature, all grown-up Ben.

"So," she said softly, running her finger along his collarbone. "I guess we should dress and go on to Ocean City."

The sheet fell back to reveal his broad, muscular chest. His was a fine specimen of man, her husband.

"Well. . . ." His deep voice hummed in her ear, reverberating through her entire body, making her shiver despite the warmth beneath the sheets. "There's no need for us to rush right off. . . ." He drew his leg over hers pulling her closer. "I mean I did pay for a whole night."

Mackenzie's lips met Ben's, her breath catching in her throat with excitement. This was all so new, so beautiful. She felt like a virgin again, just entering the world of love between a man and a woman.

"No need to rush," she repeated as he brushed his hand across her breast, sending a shudder of pleasure down her spine.

Then she closed her eyes and lost herself to the touch, smell, and taste of her new husband.

"Oh my gosh, Ben, it's beautiful!" Mackenzie exclaimed, standing on the balcony of their hotel room in Ocean City.

They'd made love not once, but twice more before they finally slipped out of the Motel 6, giggling like teenagers. Twice more! Mackenzie couldn't believe the man's stamina.

"Aren't you cold?" Ben came out onto the balcony to drape his coat over her shoulders.

"Yes, but it's so amazing." She gazed out over the bay, watching a seagull circle and call. The sun was just beginning to set in a burning ball of yellow and gold gases against the blue-gray haze of the winter sky.

Ben slipped his hand around her waist from behind her and she leaned against him. Already he smelled so familiar, so comforting.

Her grandmother had always promised her that God had someone special in mind for her. Who would have known it would be the person she'd been in love with as a girl? She smiled at the irony of it. After all those men she'd dated through the years and two long-term relationships that had soured, she had found her beloved right in her own hometown.

"Want to come inside and warm up?" He gazed over her shoulder at the brilliant sunset. "I lit the fireplace."

The room was stunningly beautiful in its simplicity and charm. Nearly shaped like a piece of pie, it had a canopy queen-size bed, a Jacuzzi large enough for the two of them, and then a living area that featured a couch, a lounge chair and a gas-burning fireplace. The room was decorated in natural shades of linen with a subtle seashell motif.

"Come on inside," he bribed. "I have champagne. . . ."

"You thought to bring champagne?"

His eyes twinkled. "And a little picnic, in case you don't feel like going out to dinner."

She let him lead her back into the room where they curled up on the couch in front of the fireplace. Ben had already set out two crystal flutes and a bottle of good champagne. There were also crackers and a small container of pâté.

"I can't believe you thought of all of this, especially with your dad being sick and all," she said, flabbergasted as she looked at the feast he'd set out on the coffee table. "It was all I could do to pack clean clothes and check on Nana this morning."

He popped the champagne cork as if he'd done it a million times and poured them both a glass. "I told you, I wanted to do everything right . . . for you, Mackenzie."

They clinked their glasses together in unison.

"To us," he said, looking her in the eyes.

"To us," she echoed, feeling as if this were some kind of dream sequence.

Ben wrapped his arm around hers, and they sipped the champagne.

The bubbles tickled Mackenzie's nose. "You even thought of food." She reached for a cracker to sample the pale-pink pâté. It was shrimp.

"And I have something for you."

She glanced up with surprise. "Something for me?"

He was smiling mischievously. "A little wedding present."

"Oh, Ben. You weren't supposed to get me a wedding present. We were going to go shopping for an engagement ring after things settled down." She exhaled. "I didn't get anything for you."

"Don't get exited before you see what it is." He reached behind him and pulled out a gift wrapped in wedding-bell paper with a big, white tulle bow. It looked like a book. He put it on her lap.

Mackenzie eyed him, wondering what on earth it could be.

"Go ahead, open it," he urged as he reached for the bottle to refill their glasses.

Mackenzie took her time, savoring the moment as she plucked off the bow and opened the paper along the seams. What could it be? A romantic book of poetry? Maybe a sensible how-to book for newly married couples?

She peeled back the paper and sucked in her breath in horrified surprise. "Oh, no, Ben, you didn't. . . ."

On her lap lay the Land's End high school yearbook from the year he had graduated.

"I found it in the attic with some of my school stuff my parents saved," he said proudly.

Either he didn't notice, or he was politely ignoring the stricken look on her face.

"Turn to page eighty-three."

She just stared at the book. She hadn't even bought one that year. She had wanted no memories of her days in high school.

Ben slid his hand over the book to open it, but she pushed it aside. "I don't want to see what I looked like then," she said carefully. "I'd just as soon not dig this up."

"Just look it up, Mackenzie. Page eighty-three."

Mackenzie was scared and she felt ridiculous for her fear. Ben had obviously already looked at her class picture and married her anyway. Why did she care now? Why couldn't she get over the past?

"Page eighty-three," he repeated. "Trust me."

Trust me. That was what marriage was about, wasn't it? She had to trust him.

When she turned to the correct page, she found, not class pictures, but class wills. Each of the graduating seniors had been invited to bequeath objects of memories to underclassmen.

There was a sticky-note flag beside the text with Ben's name.

"Read it," he said.

She skimmed through the note. He left various assorted items to underclassmen she barely recalled. Some of it made sense, some didn't. It was the last entry, though, that caught her attention.

"And to my chemistry II lab partner, Margaret, with a big thank-you for getting me through the labs and into college, I leave my favorite lab stool, my best hug, and the sincere wish that she find happiness in a world just waiting to get to know her."

Mackenzie read the sentences a second time. "This was meant for me," she finally whispered.

"You were my only lab partner."

Her Ben, she was quickly discovering, was full of surprises. He was obviously far more than the bachelor playboy everyone thought him to be. She shook her head. "I never read this."

He frowned, his forehead creasing. "You never saw it?"

"Nope. Didn't buy a yearbook."

"And none of your friends saw it?"

She glanced up at him. Her heart had started to beat again. "My friends weren't the type to buy yearbooks. Burn them, maybe, but never buy them."

He laughed. "I'm sorry I didn't recognize you when we met, but you have to admit, you look quite a bit different than you did."

"I can't believe you remembered writing this," she said, closing the book, deeply touched.

"Actually, I didn't at first," he confessed, taking the book from her. "But once I found the book and started flipping through it, I remembered."

"After you looked at my picture?"

He took her hand and kissed her knuckles. "I think you're exaggerating about how you looked."

"I'm not exaggerating."

"Okay, fine, so you're not exaggerating." He held tightly to her hand. "It's silly to argue about this. Why does it matter what you looked like?"

She sighed, meeting his gaze that would not stray.

"I don't know," she finally confessed. "It just does. It matters to me."

"Well, it doesn't matter to me." He stood and pulled her up with him. "What matters to me"—he grabbed her around the waist—"is getting my bride naked and into the Jacuzzi tub."

She laughed. The champagne had made her lightheaded. "Haven't you had enough?" she teased as their hungry mouths met.

"Enough?" He brushed her cheek with his knuckles in a tender caress. "No matter how much of you I get, Mackenzie, it will never be enough."

"I now call this emergency meeting of Bachelors Inc. to order," Owen said, bringing his fist down on Ben's kitchen table.

It was six Monday evening and Max had made them all coffee and opened a box of cookies he'd found in the cupboard.

"I don't know what you two are getting yourselves worked up about," Max grumbled, dunking his cookie in his coffee. "Can't be an official meeting anyway, 'cause you two aren't bachelors and I was never a member of your cockamamy club to begin with!"

"I can't believe Ben eloped and didn't even tell us," Zack said, sipping his coffee and grimacing. He usually drank tea. He was the one who had suggested to Owen that they needed to come over and talk to Max. Kayla swore she didn't know where Ben had gone, but when Zack called Mackenzie's office on a hunch and found out she was out of town, too, he'd put two and two together. A quick trip to the courthouse to look at public records had confirmed his suspicion. "Why wouldn't he tell us he was considering marrying her?"

"Because he was afraid you'd try to talk him out of it." Max reached for another cookie.

"That's not fair," Owen protested.

Max slurped his coffee loudly. "You saying it's not true?"

"I'm saying," Owen hemmed, "we'd have talked about it. This is an awfully sudden decision for Ben."

"Yeah," Zack agreed, "for the man who swore at my wedding less than a month ago that he would never get married."

Max shrugged. "So he met the right girl."

"*Met*, that's the operative word here," Owen said. "He just met her."

"Told me he'd known her since high school."

"*Knew* of her in high school," Owen corrected. "And then they were lab partners or some nonsense. They never even dated. Besides, that was almost twenty years ago."

Zack added more milk to his coffee. "Knowing someone when you were in high school doesn't qualify as knowing someone two decades later."

"Tell me something." Max stared Zack down until Zack felt as if he were a kid again. "When did you know your Kayla was the right woman for you?"

"What?"

"You heard me." The older man shook a bony finger. "When did you know she was the right one?"

Zack shrugged. "I realize we didn't date long before we married, but—"

"You knew she was the one the day Savannah broke her arm and you went into that hospital."

"They didn't start dating right away," Owen defended Zack.

"Only because this one was trying to ignore the obvious." Max hooked his thumb in Zack's direction. "She practically had to drag him on their first couple of dates. Practically had to hit him on the head to make him realize how much they had in common." Max slurped his coffee. "And you," he told Owen. "You went and married the same girl you went to the seventh-grade dance with." He shook his head as full of vim and vigor as he had ever been. "I'm telling you, boys, there's more to love at first sight than you young ones care to admit."

Zack glanced away. He wanted to argue Max's point, but he wasn't sure how. He *had* felt something for Kayla the first time he met her the day Savannah broke her arm, but this was different because it involved Ben. Wasn't it?

Zack took another sip of the coffee and reached for a chocolate mint cookie. "I just would have felt better if he'd talked to us first, that's all I'm saying."

"Exactly," Owen agreed. "We wouldn't have tried to talk him out of marrying her if that was what he really wanted. We would just have tried to be sure that was what he really wanted.

"Maybe put it off a few weeks," Zack interjected.

Max looked at them both. "So maybe he wanted to do this on his own. Maybe he wanted to do it without having you help him make the decision."

Zack and Owen were quiet for a moment. Zack truly did wish Ben all the happiness in the world. He wanted him to be as happy as he was, and Zack knew in his heart that Kayla had made the difference in his life. But Ben Gordon, the girl magnet, married? He was just having a difficult time imagining it.

"Well," Owen said getting up from the table. "We better go and let you get some rest."

"Get some rest?" Max gave a laugh. "I feel better than I've felt in years. Myrtle's coming over shortly to snuggle up on the couch with me and watch a John Wayne movie."

"Which one?" Zack got up, taking his cup to the sink.

"*Green Berets*. Want to stay and watch?"

Zack smiled. He liked Max immensely and had a great deal of respect for him. "No, thanks. Wouldn't want to move in on your hot date."

Owen put his cup in the sink, too. "Speaking of Myrtle and hot dates, you've been with this woman more than two weeks." He looked at Max slyly. "You going to be making an important announcement of your own shortly?"

Max dunked his last cookie into his coffee. "I don't know, boys." He studied the wet cookie, musing. "I like Myrtle a hell of a lot but. . . ." He let his voice trail off.

"Well, you take care of yourself." Zack patted him on the shoulder. "And you call us if you have so much as a stomachache. Kayla said she'd be happy to stay the night with you."

"I don't need a baby-sitter." He winked. "Besides, I might have a little sleepover of my own."

Zack was still laughing when he climbed into his VW microbus and pulled out of the driveway.

Fifteen

"You guys don't look surprised." Ben opened his arms wide, trying to hide his disappointment as he turned to Mackenzie. "They don't look surprised," he told her, keeping his tone light. And they don't look happy, he thought.

Ben was happy and he wanted Zack and Owen to be happy, too. Happy for him. He and Mackenzie had returned to Land's End that afternoon and invited the guys and their wives over for dinner. He'd made seafood scampi and everything. He wanted to have everyone gathered together so he and Mackenzie could tell them together.

He looked at his friends seated on his couch and on the carpet in his newly painted living room. They were looking at him, half smiles plastered on their faces.

"Pop, did you blow the surprise?" he asked Max.

Max had turned down the invitation to join them, but hung in the kitchen doorway eavesdropping.

Max threw his hands up in self-defense. "Not me. I didn't tell anyone, not even Myrtle."

"Actually, we kind of guessed," Zack confessed sheepishly from his place on the floor in front of the coffee table. "And then I went downtown to check the court records just to be sure."

Kayla, also seated on the floor, rested a hand on her husband's leg. "I didn't tell, Ben. Didn't tell because I didn't know." Then she smiled slyly. At least she seemed pleased. "At least I didn't know for sure."

Ben collapsed in the love seat beside his new wife, throwing his hands up in surrender. "I give up. I've never been able to have secrets from these guys."

Mackenzie chuckled good-naturedly. He loved her smile, loved the thought that he had something to do with that smile.

"So it's not a surprise," she said patting his thigh as if they'd been man and wife for years and not just a little longer than a day. "That doesn't mean we're not still married."

Abby laughed. "She's right. And actually we are surprised."

"Shocked is a better word," Owen said.

"Why?" Ben took Mackenzie's hand in his, entwining his fingers with hers.

Zack tugged on his ponytail. "*Why*, you ask?"

"Maybe because you were the world's biggest self-proclaimed bachelor until sometime yesterday." Abby ran her hand over her rounding abdomen. "A couple of weeks ago at Zack and Kayla's wedding I specifically remember you offering a toast to all the bachelors left in the world, including yourself."

He glanced at Mackenzie. He had nothing to hide; she knew what he was. What he had been, at least. "So I met the right woman."

"Just what I said," Max offered from the doorway. "Who wants cake and coffee? Looks like a wedding cake in here on the counter."

"A wedding cake?" Mackenzie met Abby's and Kayla's gazes. "Oh, you guys, thanks."

"You're welcome," Kayla said with a smile. Then to Max, "Just a small sliver. But after that, we've got to go. We're supposed to pick Savannah up at the school at eight."

"Just a sliver for me," Zack called.

"Cake for us, but no coffee," Owen answered for himself and Abby.

"I'll have cake, too." Mackenzie rose, tucking blond hair behind her ear. He loved it when she wore her hair down like this. "I'll help. You want cake, Ben?"

Seeing her standing there in a pair of jeans and a thin white sweater brought a sweat to his brow. All he could think of was that he wanted their guests to have their cake and go home so he could have Mackenzie to himself. "Um, sure. Cake would be great," he managed.

She flashed him a smile that told him she knew what he was thinking.

Everyone had their cake and coffee and finally took their leave, offering congratulations as they went. When the last one had pulled out of the driveway, Ben flipped the outside lights off and he and Mackenzie returned to the living room to clean up the dishes. Owen and Abby had offered to stay and help, but Ben had been so anxious to get them out of the house, that he had refused any help.

"Guess I'll mosey on to bed if you don't need me," Max said from the far side of the room.

"Don't need a thing, Pop. Thanks for help with dinner tonight."

Mackenzie stood near his dad, her thumbs hooked in her jean pockets. "Yeah, thanks, Max. We appreciate your support through all this. I mean that."

Max took a step toward his new daughter-in-law and gave her a hug. She hugged him back. "Just glad to have you in the family," Max said, his voice filled with emotion. "Glad Ben found a good woman to keep him straight."

When Max pulled away, he was grinning, but there were tears in his eyes.

"Just holler if you need anything, Dad."

Max lifted a hand as he went down the hallway. "See you in the morning."

Ben made himself wait until his father closed his bedroom door to run up behind Mackenzie and throw his arms around her. She was picking up dirty dessert plates.

"Ben! Careful or I'm going to drop everything," she protested, not really meaning it, as he lifted her off her feet.

She was solid muscle and well toned. She had an exquisite body that was both athletic and feminine at the same time. Ben had never made love to a woman who was as beautiful as Mackenzie. Never wanted a woman again and again as he wanted her.

"So put down the dishes and give me a kiss," he told her.

She set down the plates and turned in his arms to face him. "I think that went okay," she said.

He frowned. "They weren't surprised. I suppose it was silly to try to surprise them." He exhaled.

"And I'm afraid they're hurt I didn't tell them ahead of time."

"I don't think so," she answered thoughtfully. "I think maybe they understood why we did it this way." She stroked his cheek. "They're good people, Ben. Good friends"

"They are," he agreed. "I'm just glad they know how to take a hint and hit the road."

She laughed, meeting his mouth with hers. "Take the hint? How could they miss it? You practically tossed them out on their ears," she laughed.

He kissed her neck, tracing an imaginary line to her collarbone with his lips. "I'm awfully tired. You tired?"

She pushed him away playfully and picked up the dirty dishes.

He grabbed a pile and followed her to the kitchen.

"It's only eight o'clock. We can't go to bed at eight o'clock." She placed the dishes in the sink and began to rinse them off.

He took the wet plates and loaded them in the dishwasher. He knew her well enough to know it would be easier getting her to bed if the kitchen was cleaned up. "Why is that too early to go to bed? It's my house, my bed. I can go to bed when I want to."

"What's your dad going to think?"

He met her gaze, his eyes twinkling. "He'll think I'm anxious to get naked under the covers with my new wife, that's what he'll think."

She blushed and turned away. Luckily, he knew she enjoyed their lovemaking as much as he did.

"You're so bad," she said.

"And you love it."

She turned back to him with a smile. He really loved the fact that she was tall, that she could look him right in the eye like this. "You're right. I do love it," she said. "And I love you."

They kissed, wet, dirty dishes between them.

"Okay, make you a deal," Ben said. "You finish up here, I'll check on Dad and meet you in the bedroom in five minutes."

"Deal," she agreed as Ben hurried out of the kitchen, thankful he'd had the good sense to put his father's bedroom on the first floor and his own in the loft on the second.

"Magee's Flower Shop, tree number three," Mackenzie said, peering over her tortoise-shell reading glasses at the young woman standing in front of her.

"Thanks," the woman said.

"No problem." Mackenzie checked off Magee's on her list of sponsors on her clipboard. She'd been checking in sponsors for half an hour. The hall of the church was already bustling with activity as people came and went with boxes and bags of decorations for their trees.

"Next," Mackenzie called, without glancing up. Only a dozen more sponsors to check in and she could get to work on her own tree.

"Land's End Renovations," came Ben's rich tenor voice.

She glanced up with a grin, trying not to think about their lovemaking last night and again this morning before they headed off for work. "Hey, hon."

"Hi." He gave her a quick husbandly kiss.

All around her, Mackenzie heard the room buzzing. Word was already getting around town that Land's End's number one bachelor had wed. In a small town with a low crime rate and nearly a hundred percent employment, it was apparently news worthy of gossip and consternation.

Mackenzie glanced at her clipboard. "Your trees are twenty-one and thirty-two." She pointed. "The first one is down toward the end of the first row. The second tree is a third of the way down in the second row"

"Thanks."

He picked up a cardboard box that was taped shut so she couldn't see what kind of ornaments her husband had bought, made, or stolen.

"How long you going to be here?" he asked.

She surveyed the line. Hopefully everyone was here and accounted for. "Not long. Want me to help you decorate?"

He frowned. "I do not. And I don't want you scoping me out either. I told you I can handle this myself and I can. I'll find you when I'm done."

Chuckling, she glanced down at her clipboard. "If you say so. See you later."

Ben went into the church hall to find his trees and Mackenzie finished checking the rest of the sponsors in. Everyone was accounted for but one and a call from her cell phone confirmed that someone would be coming to decorate that last tree; he'd just had a flat tire and was running late. Once everyone was checked in and extra extension cords were located, Mackenzie went out to her car to get her box of carved bird ornaments. All of the trees already had lights on them, a gift from a local hardware store, so she was able to get right to decorating her tree. In an hour, she had her carved wooden birds placed just where she wanted them, tiny nests here and there and the tree trimmed with wisps of brown raffia garland. When she stepped back to look at the seven-foot tree, she had to admit it was beautiful in its simplicity.

Her tree decorated, Mackenzie began to walk through the forest of fresh green Christmas trees, looking to see how others were decorated. Though she already knew most of the themes of the trees, she was still overwhelmed by their beauty and the creativity of those who decorated them. There was a tree laden with angels, a tree of elves, a tree of trains, complete with a locomotive that circled the tree skirt, and even a tree with tiny cookies, pastries and rolling pins. Though she was sorely tempted each time she drew near one of Ben's trees, she turned away, wanting to save the surprise to share with him.

"Congratulations," a woman said, offering her hand to Mackenzie. "Sandy Phillips, Delmarva Radiology."

"Nice to meet you." Mackenzie shook her hand.

Delmarva Radiology had a cute tree that featured little bones, tiny X rays, and even miniature casts and crutches. Their tree was always a big hit, Mackenzie had been told, and always went for a high bid to one of the medical offices in town.

"I'm Mackenzie Say—Mackenzie Gordon," she corrected herself.

"So I hear." Sandy was smiling. She obviously knew Ben; everyone knew Ben.

Not sure what to say, Mackenzie studied the tree she was finishing. "This is so neat." She fingered a tiny crutch. "Who makes all of these things?"

"A couple of our patients," Sandy said, obviously looking Mackenzie over. She lowered her voice. "So I have to ask. Everyone else is dying to know."

Mackenzie glanced up, not sure she was following the conversation.

Sandy touched her arm and got very close, as if they were great confidantes. "How'd you do it? How'd you trap the great Ben Gordon into marriage?" she asked in a hushed tone. "Someone said you were pregnant, but I said that's too obvious."

Mackenzie stared at the woman for a second, not sure what to say. She didn't like what the woman was insinuating. She hadn't *trapped* Ben. Ben wasn't the kind of man that anyone trapped into doing anything, and if Sandy the radiologist really knew him, she would know that.

Mackenzie looked down into the woman's eyes. "We were in love," she said flatly. "He wanted to get married."

"He wanted to get married?" she asked wide-eyed, almost dazed with surprise.

Mackenzie smiled woodenly, holding up a finger. "Could you excuse me? I think someone is calling me." She hurried away, wishing she could run straight for the exit sign.

Mackenzie didn't stop until she reached the ladies' room, where she splashed some water on her face. As she looked up, a woman exited one of the stalls.

"Hi," the woman said. She looked to be in her late thirties, early forties, dressed in a sweatsuit with her hair pulled back in a ponytail. "You're Mackenzie, Ben's new wife, right?"

Mackenzie glanced at her in the mirror, wary. "Yes, I am. Mackenzie Sayer Gordon. I have the new painting company in town. I'm chairing the committee this year." She gestured toward the door and the commotion in the hall.

"Nice to meet you." The woman thrust her hands under a water faucet. "Kay Rawlins." She smiled at Mackenzie in the mirror. "Quite the romantic man you have there."

Mackenzie gave a half smile. "He is, but why do you say so?"

"The tree," Kay said.

"Oh, his tree." She smiled sheepishly. "Actually I haven't seen them yet. He wanted to surprise me."

"Well, I won't tell you and spoil the surprise." The woman grabbed a paper towel and began to dry her hands as she headed out the door. "But I have to say, you're the envy of every woman in that room tonight. Probably every woman in Land's End."

Kay went out the bathroom door and Mackenzie reached for a towel to dry her own hands. She'd been curious all evening as to what Ben had done to his trees, but now she was beside herself with curiosity. Something romantic? How could a Christmas tree be romantic?

Mackenzie walked out the bathroom door, practically running into Ben.

"There you are!" He grabbed her and kissed her. "I've been looking for you." He was grinning ear to ear.

"So, are you done?" she asked, not wanting him to know just how anxious she was to see his trees.

"I'm done. Ready to see them?"

"Ready."

He looped his arm through hers and led her back into the main hall, which had been transformed into a winter wonderland in a matter of hours. "First the boring tree," he told her, escorting her on his arm down the aisle of trees as if they were in a church sanctuary. "Then the surprise."

"The romantic one?" she said.

He frowned. "They didn't tell you, did they? I made everyone swear they wouldn't tell you."

She smoothed his arm, unable to help but notice the muscle beneath her fingertips. "No one told me a thing, except that you must be very romantic and that I must be very lucky or very conniving to have tricked you into marriage."

He laughed, seeming unconcerned that someone would accuse her of such treachery. "Okay, tree number one." He stopped in front of his first tree.

She brought her hands to her cheeks in delight. The tree was decorated with tiny tools; hammers, saws, screwdrivers, even little pliers. The garland was made from red measuring tape.

"Ben! It's beautiful!" she laughed. "Where did you find all of the little tools?" She walked around the tree, studying the tiny tools with amazement.

"Toy store." He was obviously pleased with himself. "I know, who wants tools on their Christmas tree? But—"

"No, no, we have a lot of businesses that buy these trees. People even come from Annapolis. We'll sell it easily."

He crossed his arms over his chest. "So you like it?"

She kissed his cheek. "I like it."

"Now the other one?" he asked.

She nodded and Ben took her arm once again and led her through the forest of twinkling trees. Despite the crowd of milling people and those who watched them with curiosity, it was fun to walk through the trees, taking notice of various decorations as they made their way to Ben's other tree.

He stopped as they neared his tree. "Close your eyes."

"What?" She was laughing. She hadn't laughed as much in her life as she'd laughed with Ben in the last three weeks.

"Close your eyes. I'll lead you so you don't trip over the extension cords or anything."

She closed her eyes and let him lead her to his tree. He halted and turned her shoulders so that she was obviously facing it. He stood behind her and placed his hands over her eyes. He smelled of pine and his musky aftershave. A heavenly combination. "Ready?"

"Yes, I'm ready!" She was so ready, she was about to burst.

He pulled his hands away and Mackenzie sucked in her breath.

White and gold. The tree was all in white and

gold with wedding bands everywhere. Wedding bands and white doves and ringlets of metallic gold and iridescent white ribbon. It was simple in design, yet shockingly exquisite. "Oh, Ben," was all she could muster.

"I call it the wedding tree. I know, very original. I thought I'd bid on it myself. It would look great in our newly painted living room." Mackenzie turned and threw her arms around him, burying her face in his shoulder. People had gathered around to watch her reaction and now they were all talking at once.

She kept her eyes shut, her face nestled in his navy blue sweater so no one would see her tears. "Thank you," she whispered, too emotional to say more. "It's the most beautiful Christmas tree I've ever seen."

"Glad you like it." He kissed the top of her head, stroking her back "Merry Christmas, sweetheart."

Sixteen

"Hey, Mackenzie?"

She stepped out of the master bathroom she and Ben shared, into the bedroom where he was dressing. She held her toothbrush in her hand. "Yes?" she asked, feeling tired, though she had just gotten up.

Mackenzie supposed all honeymoon periods had to end and reality had to set in. But in the two months since Ben had bought his wedding tree and her bird tree at the auction and they had celebrated Christmas with two trees in the living room, reality had offered no clues as to why she had become so edgy and sensitive. Lately, it seemed as if everything Ben said or did touched a nerve, even though he hadn't changed at all. He was still sweet and considerate and loving. So, what was wrong? What was wrong with her?

"Do you think you can make dinner tonight at six-thirty at Angelo's? It's with a prospective client." Ben buttoned up an oxford shirt as he came around the king-size waterbed.

She paused before answering because it was one of the ways her grandmother had taught her one person showed respect for another, even when irritated. "Six-thirty, Ben?"

"I know, your grandmother," he said, sounding completely understanding. "But it's important. We really need this job."

"We really need all of them," she muttered under her breath, stepping back into the bathroom in her panties and bra to brush her teeth.

"What was that?"

"Nothing, dear."

He didn't have a clue she was annoyed. Not a clue.

It was funny how none of the things she had feared would be a problem in the marriage had come to pass. Ben's relationship with Zack and Owen never got in the way. He saw and talked to his friends often, yet they never made her feel she was being short-changed by their friendship. And Max, living right under the same roof with them, never interfered or made her feel unwelcome in the home that was his as well as his son's. In fact, in the last week or so, Ben's father had actually acted as a buffer between her and Ben on more than one occasion.

Now that the initial honeymoon period was over and it was early February, the oddest things about Ben were beginning to annoy her.

She reached for the toothpaste cap on the sink and crammed it on the toothpaste. He never put the toothpaste lid back on, and he never did his laundry until every stitch of clothing in the house was dirty.

Mackenzie studied her face in the mirror as she brushed her teeth vigorously. Maybe the stress of their two businesses was just getting her down. After all, she had known she and Ben would hit little bumps in the road once the newness of the marriage had worn off. She had just hoped it wouldn't be quite so soon. Ben was certainly still warm and attentive, but he never paid attention to the little details that were important to her. Of course, he expected her to pay attention to the details that mattered to him.

Rinsing out her mouth, she dropped her toothbrush back in the holder. Maybe Max was right. The other night she'd grumbled about Ben not shopping for his night to cook until an hour before they were supposed to eat. She usually didn't share such complaints with Max because she didn't think it was right, but she'd been so annoyed that she hadn't been able to hold back.

"Just two bachelors trying to adjust to each other is all it is," Max had told her with a kind pat on her shoulder. "You two lived alone a lot of years and it takes time to accept change."

She certainly hoped that was all it was, she thought glumly.

Flipping off the bathroom light, Mackenzie went into the bedroom to dress. Ben had already made the bed and Howie was stretched out on it, sound asleep. If nothing else, the dog was adjusting well to the marriage.

Ben sat on the edge of the bed to put on his work boots. She went to her dresser to pull out khakis and sweater.

"Is that a yes?" he asked sweetly, meaning the dinner plans. The man had a one-track mind, and he never gave up or gave in until he got what he wanted.

"Yes," she conceded with a sigh. It wasn't that she didn't want to help him with his business, it was just that they were both working such long hours. Some time home alone together would have been nice. "I'll come home and change clothes, stop at the nursing home, and meet you at the restaurant." She pulled her sweater over her head. "All right?"

"Perfect." He started for the door to go make coffee for them both as he did every morning. "Oh, and if you could, hon, would you wear the red dress?"

She glanced up at him, unable to suppress her surprised annoyance. He wanted to tell her how to dress? She lifted an eyebrow. "I have to wear the red dress?"

He flashed her the killer grin he knew she found hard to resist, even when she knew he was using it to get to her. "No, of course you don't have to wear it. Wear whatever you want. It's just that you always look so hot in that dress." He walked out the door. "Coffee will be up in a sec."

Her khakis pulled up one leg, Mackenzie stared at the door Ben had just walked through. Was he serious? Did he want her to wear something to impress a potential client?

She shoved her other leg into her pants and pulled them up. No, she would not wear the red dress. Not if it was the last dress left on this planet!

* * *

Mackenzie parked her old Porche and climbed out of the car. It was bitter cold out and there was snow in the forecast again.

Angelo's bright twinkling lights shone through window and onto the street. She was half an hour late. She'd been running late all day, and then had changed clothes three times. In the end, she had decided to wear the red dress. Now that she was here, she wished she hadn't.

Mackenzie went into the restaurant and left her coat in the coatroom. The hostess pointed her in the direction of Ben's table, but he spotted her and was out of his chair in an instant.

"Sweetheart." He came to her, taking her arm, kissing her hello.

"I'm sorry I'm late," she said, now sorry she'd been angry with him all day long. Most women would kill to have their husbands give them the attention Ben gave her.

"You look great." He ran his blue-eyed gaze over her, as if imagining what she looked like without it, and kissed her again.

She glanced down at the floor, feeling petty, glad she had worn the dress. It was the least she could do. It wasn't as if he asked much of her.

"Come meet Mr. Carol." He took her arm and steered her in the direction he'd come. "He's interested in restoring several of those little 1920s bungalows on the west end of Cedar Drive and then selling them. You know the ones I mean?"

Dinner went fine with the investor from Annapolis, and Mackenzie and Ben were home in bed by ten-thirty. She sat up in bed, paperwork propped on her knees as she went over some bids. Ben was reading a new suspense novel. He put a bookmark in his book, set it on the nightstand, and rolled onto his side to face her.

"Thanks for coming tonight." He ran his hand over her leg. She was wearing powder-blue silk pajamas, one of the many gifts he had bestowed upon her since their wedding day. "I knew you could help me sell Carol on my ideas." He chuckled. "I knew the dress would sell him if I couldn't."

She glanced at him over the rim of her glasses. Again, she felt a bubble of annoyance. She knew he was complimenting her, but she didn't like the way it sounded. "I could have helped make the sale wearing my painting coveralls, too," she told him.

He looked at her as if he didn't get it. "I know you could have, hon."

She glanced back at the paperwork in her lap. She needed to get through it all tonight, but she was so tired that the numbers were all beginning to run together.

Ben was quiet for a moment, but he was watching her. Irritating her. "Something wrong, Mackenzie?" he finally asked.

She paused. She knew she was being petty. Here her husband was complimenting her on her business abilities and her appearance, and she was ticked off with him. "No," she sighed, setting the paperwork on the table beside the bed. She pulled off her glasses and rubbed her eyes. "I'm just tired. My head hurts."

"I know just the cure for a headache." He reached out to her. "Lie back and I'll give you a massage."

She considered protesting. She didn't want sex right now. She wanted to just lie here with her throbbing headache and go over all the ways her perfect husband annoyed her.

She slid down in the bed, closing her eyes. He was already stroking her through her pajamas, his hands moving in small, mesmerizing circles. "Mmmm," she hummed as she felt the tension in her body begin to ease against her will.

"Want to take off the pj's?" he asked. "It works better without clothes."

She wanted to argue, but already she was beginning to feel better. Just the touch of his hands seemed to have a calming affect. Mackenzie slipped out of her pajamas and stretched out on the bed on her back, her eyes closed.

Ben took his time, kneading every tired muscle in her body, working downward from her shoulders to her toes. He ran his hands through her hair, massaging her scalp, rubbing her temples in slow, purposeful circular motions. He took each of her feet, one at a time, in his lap and massaged the balls, the heels, every toe. He rolled her onto her stomach and massaged her calves, her buttocks, her back and shoulders. He must have worked ten minutes on her neck.

Mackenzie could feel the stress of the day melting, washing away with the pressure of his magical hands.

Finished with her back, he rolled her over again. She felt as if she were drifting on a cloud, warm and relaxed.

Again, he began to stroke her legs, his strokes slightly different. He rubbed hard, then gently. Tingles of pleasure began to radiate from her stomach. Lying on his side, facing her, he worked his way slowly up her legs, paying careful attention to the soft, tender flesh of her inner thighs.

"Mmm," she sighed, only now her sighs were beginning to sound like moans.

Maybe making love before they went to sleep wasn't such a bad idea after all. . . .

He continued to stroke and she naturally parted her thighs.

Ben leaned over and kissed her breast. Her nipple puckered in immediate response.

He continued to stoke, moving upward to the apex of her thighs. Delicious, unhurried, warm strokes. . . .

Mackenzie was growing warmer by the minute. As his strokes became slower, more localized, she found herself moving against him.

He leaned over and took her nipple in his warm mouth, eliciting another moan from deep in her throat.

She was damp now, damp and achy. She moved to the rhythm of his hand, thoroughly enjoying his unhurried attention. That was one of the things Mackenzie loved about the way Ben made love to her. He always acted as if he had all the time in the world. He always made it a point to see she was satisfied before he took his own pleasure.

Ben eased Mackenzie in his arms so that her head rested on his shoulder. She rested her leg on his hip.

His hand moved deeper, his fingers exploring the soft, dampness of her most sensitive flesh.

Mackenzie could feel her breath growing short as she moved faster against his hand. The troubles at work, the toothpaste cap, even the red dress, faded from her memory. Now all that mattered was the smell of Ben's hair, the feel of his hand, and the taste of her desire.

Ben knew her body and played it well. Again and again, he stroked her to the near point of orgasm, only to back off just a little bit. Then he would build her up again. Her breath shortened to pants. She could feel the sweat on her brow. She strained against him and sensing her urgency, he stroked faster.

Mackenzie's world burst in bright twinkling lights of pleasure. Every muscle in her body seemed to tense and relax as aftershocks of delight rippled through her.

Ben held her in his arms and covered her face with soft, gentle kisses. When she could breathe again, she opened her eyes, looked into his. He had made no attempt to move to the next stage of their lovemaking. She ran her hand over his side, down his hip. "Don't you want to. . . . ?"

"Nah," he murmured in her ear. "You're tired and your head hurts." He closed his eyes, snuggling against her. "Let's just shut out the light and go to sleep."

Still floating on the last wisps of pleasure, she reached over and shut out the light. Ben pulled her into his arms again and she rested her head on his shoulder and drifted off to sleep.

A few days later Mackenzie stood in line with Ben at the local lumberyard. He had to pick up some materials for Zack and she had to get spackling equipment, so they decided to ride over together.

They'd deliver Zack's materials to the site in her van and then she would drop Ben back off at home.

As they waited, they went over their plans for the day. Mackenzie had a Chamber of Commerce meeting tonight, so she wanted to stop and see Nana before she went to the meeting. Howie had a vet's appointment at five, so Ben was going to take care of that.

When the salesclerk starting ringing up the items on their cart, Mackenzie put up her hand. "That's all. It's two separate bills. I'm sorry. I should have told you."

Ben already had his credit card out of his pocket. "It's okay," he told the clerk. "I'll pay for it all."

She looked at him. "No, you will not." She eyed the salesclerk. "Just ring up his stuff and I'll pay for my own."

"Mackenzie—"

"Ben. It's my company." She tried to keep the irritation out of her voice. "I pay for my own supplies. We keep our books separate. That was the deal."

"Hon, I'll give you the receipt—"

She snatched the credit card out of Ben's hand and handed it to the clerk. "They'll be paid for separately."

Ben gave the girl one of his smiles. "My new wife is both lovely and independent, as you can see."

"Oh," she flirted as she ran the card through the cash register. "You're newlyweds."

"Two months," he said proudly.

Mackenzie looked at her watch, and then at the clerk.

Getting the hint, the girl handed Ben his card and the receipt. "Thank you, Mr. Gordon. Have a nice day."

Outside at the van, Mackenzie tossed Ben the keys. Without waiting for his help, she began to unload the cart into the back of the van. She was angry with him again and didn't want to be. In the last few weeks she had begun to take notice of just how often he mentioned her appearance, to her, to others. She was beginning to feel like the trophy wife rather than his marriage partner.

"I guess you don't want help," Ben said, standing behind her and she practically threw a pack of rollers into the back of the utility van.

"I hate having to come buy this stuff when the orders don't come in on time," she said.

He watched her, a strange look on his face, almost as if he didn't quite recognize who she was.

"You know, it costs more money to do this retail," she told him. "Even with my contractor's discount this is an expensive way to do business." She took the keys from his hand and walked around to the driver's side.

Ben hopped in the passenger side, watching her.

She slipped on her seat belt and pulled out of the parking lot.

"Mackenzie, is there something wrong?"

She kept her gaze on the road. "I'm just irritated that I had to do this today. I have a lot of work to get done."

"I mean me. Is there something wrong with me or how I'm doing something?"

She gripped the steering wheel. She didn't really

want to talk about this now. Didn't want to talk about it at all if she could help it.

"I'm just wondering," he said when she didn't answer. "Because lately you've been a little edgy with me. I thought maybe you were angry."

"I'm not angry," she said a little too firmly.

Out of the corner of her eye, she could almost see him pull back from her.

"I'm not angry," she said more gently this time. "Just . . . just stressed out."

"And it's not me that's stressing you out?"

She glanced at him, then back at the road. "Could you please put the toothpaste cap back on the toothpaste?"

"Sure." He gave her one of those I-have-no-clue-what-you're-talking-about laughs. "Anything else?"

She looked at him again. "Why didn't you go to the prom with me when I asked you?"

"What?"

She signaled and pulled into the development where Zack was working. Owen was supposed to meet them there as well. Something about some changes to the floor plan of an addition.

"Why didn't you go to the prom with me?" she repeated.

"You're angry because I leave the cap off the toothpaste and I didn't go to a prom with you?" She could hear the irritation in his voice now. "A prom that at this moment I can't remember who I *did* go with?"

"Never mind," she said, seeing Zack's van parked in a driveway up ahead.

"Mackenzie—"

She pulled into the driveway, hitting the brakes a little harder than she intended and jumped out.

"Mackenzie." Ben got out of her van and came around to the back.

She pulled open the doors and began to slide out the planks he had purchased.

"Hey, guys!" Owen appeared around the end of the van, a mug in his hand. "How's it going?" He sipped his coffee. "Zack's inside. Need a hand?"

Mackenzie unceremoniously dropped two quarts of stain into his arms.

Owen glanced at Ben, lifting a brow. Ben shrugged.

Mackenzie ignored them.

Ben pulled the lumber out of the van, and she shut the doors. "I have to get to a job site. Will you give Ben a ride back to the house when you guys are done here, Owen?"

Again, Owen looked at Ben. Both men were avoiding eye contact with her now.

"Sure. No problem."

"Well, then I guess I'll see you tonight for dinner?" Ben said to her.

She nodded. "See you tonight."

Ben and Owen stepped out of the way as Mackenzie threw the van into reverse. The two men stood in the driveway watching her pull away.

"So, buddy," Owen said with amusement. "I take it the bloom is off the honeymoon rose?"

Seventeen

Ben watched Mackenzie pull away in her van, still unsure as to what just happened. "I don't know. I guess," he mumbled as much to himself as to Owen.

The two men headed toward the house, lumber and cans of stain in hand. "So, what did you do? And please don't tell me it's the toilet seat issue. We warned you."

"I don't know what's wrong," Ben exclaimed in frustration. "That's the problem. I don't know what I did and she won't tell me." They walked around the back of the house to the tarpapered new addition. "She's not making any sense. First, she got angry because I was trying to save time by putting her stuff on my bill at the lumberyard this morning. Then when I ask her what's wrong, she comes out of the blue saying she doesn't want me to leave the cap off the toothpaste."

Owen laughed. "I got chewed out yesterday morning for asking for cash." He shrugged. "What's the sense in both of us going to the money machine?"

Ben carried the wood through the door Zack was

holding open for him. "Oh, it gets better. Next she asks me why I didn't go to the prom with her."

Owen passed Zack at the door. "Bloom's off the rose," he told Zack. "Honeymoon's come to a screeching halt."

"Dirty underwear on the floor?" Zack asked, entirely serious for once.

"He doesn't know," Owen said.

Zack closed the door behind them. "He doesn't know?"

Ben leaned the lumber against a wall beam. "I don't know."

Zack and Owen stood facing Ben as all three men tried to think the situation through carefully.

"Sex is good?" Zack asked.

"Great."

Owen scratched his chin. "Enough snuggling, kissing, telling her she looks good, not just thinking it."

Ben had been so happy these last weeks since he and Mackenzie got married. Happier than he could have believed possible and he knew that she was happy. Yet, suddenly she was miserable, and he didn't know how to make it better. "I've done plenty of that stuff, except the compliments." He held up a finger, stuffing his other hand in his coat pocket. Despite the space heater, it was cold in the addition. "She's touchy about compliments. I have to be very careful."

"And she doesn't want to talk about what's wrong?" Zack asked.

Ben shook his head. "So far, no. What I just heard in the van on the way over here is the most she's said." He glanced morosely out the window at the wintry garden. "Now with this prom thing, I'm even more confused."

"That's strange that she doesn't want to talk about it," Zack mused. "Usually it's the women who want to talk things out and the men who go silent."

Owen crossed his arms over his chest. "So just out of curiosity, why didn't you go to the prom with her?"

Ben shrugged. "I don't know." He tried to think back. "Who the hell did I go with?"

Zack shook his finger. "Hillary Rosenbleum," he said with a grin. "I remember distinctly that it was big-chested Hillary."

Ben couldn't even remember her face, or her chest for that matter, but the name rang a bell. "That's right." He shrugged. "I don't know why I didn't go with her. I guess I'd already asked Hillary."

Zack began to examine the planks Ben had brought in. "I don't know, buddy. Somehow there's a connection between the toothpaste cap and the prom. You've just got to figure it out."

Ben sighed. He appreciated Zack's and Owen's help, even if they hadn't come to any conclusions. It helped knowing they had been through this kind of thing with their own wives. "Well, hey, don't worry about us. We'll be fine. We'll get it right. You know how it is, adjusting to someone living with you in your bedroom." He met Owen's gaze. "I'll make it work," he told him firmly.

Owen gave him a slap on the shoulder as he walked by. "Just let us know if we can help."

* * *

When Mackenzie arrived home from the Chamber of Commerce meeting, Ben was already there. He met her at the door, took an armload of stuff out of her hands, and carried it into the living room. "I made some pasta. Hungry?"

"Tired," she sighed. She *was* tired. Tired and upset. She didn't know where that question about the prom came from today. That happened twenty years ago, a lifetime. It was unfair to Ben, unfair to their relationship. The problem was that, while she could come to that conclusion mentally, emotionally she was still upset with him.

"You need to eat something," Ben said. "How about we have some salad and pasta and I'll run the tub for you."

He was being so sweet. So why was she still pissed?

She met his gaze in the dark living room. "I'm sorry about this morning. I was trying to start a fight and I don't even know why."

He set her notebooks and leather backpack on the couch and gave her a hug. "Forgiven." He kissed her lightly on the lips and grabbed her hand. "Come on now or the pasta will get cold."

"Where's Dad?" She followed him into the kitchen. She didn't know when she had started calling Max Dad; she'd just gotten up one morning and realized she was doing it. It was nice to call someone Dad, seeing as she'd never had one of her own.

"He and Myrtle went out to dinner and then to square dancing."

The table was already set. She went to get water glasses and fill them up. "Think this is getting serious between your dad and the Turtle?"

"I don't know." He drained the pasta. "He's been saying all along he wanted to remarry. I suppose it's a possibility. He's never dated anyone else this long."

Mackenzie brought the plates to the stove and Ben put some pasta on each. She added the marinara sauce he'd prepared and walked back to the table. Ben grabbed the salad out of the refrigerator and sat beside her.

Mackenzie blessed the meal for them both and reached for salad. As they made their way through the busywork of preparing their plates, they were silent.

Ben took a bite of pasta, then set down his fork. "Okay, I have to ask. What was with the prom question? I didn't even remember who I went with until the guys reminded me."

She glanced up, immediately feeling defensive. "I don't know. I just wanted to know why you didn't go with me when I asked you."

"Mackenzie, that was so long ago."

She could tell he was getting frustrated with her. She wondered if she ought to just let it drop. After all, these were *her* insecurities, weren't they *her* problem?

"Say something," he said finally.

"What?" She set down her fork loudly. "What do you want me to say? I wanted to know why you didn't go with me, that's all."

"I don't know," he answered raising his voice a notch. "I don't remember. I guess because I'd already invited Hillary Rosenbleum."

She stared at her plate. Now neither was eating.

She wished she'd just kept her mouth shut. "Not because I was fat?"

He groaned. "You were not—" He halted in midsentence and started again. "I'm not getting into this fat conversation with you again. It's very simple. I didn't go out with you because I already had a date."

She remained quiet, feeling tears burn in the back of her eyelids.

"Well?" he said. "Is that a satisfactory answer?"

When she didn't answer, he got up from the table. "I'm not hungry," he said and walked away. "I'll be in my office if you need me."

Mackenzie was able to hold back the tears, but only long enough for him to get out of the room.

Max came in later than usual that night, but Ben was still up, working in his office. Mackenzie had stopped in earlier to say good night. They'd both apologized for their behavior, but Ben still felt lousy. Their apologies were just smoothing over the surface, but he knew a big problem lay underneath; he just didn't know what it was.

"Still up?" Max asked as Ben came down the stairs to let Howie out once more before bed.

"Doing some late work," Ben answered glumly. He went into the kitchen to let the dog out the back door.

Max followed, going to the refrigerator for a glass of milk.

"So how was your date?" Ben leaned against the counter. He was so tired that his eyes were achy and scratchy. He needed to go to bed; he just wasn't quite ready to face the chill that he feared would be in the bedroom.

"It was good." Max nodded. "All right," he amended.

"Just all right?" Ben massaged the bridge of his nose. "I thought you really liked Myrtle."

"I do." Max sipped his milk, leaning over a chair to glance at the newspaper left on the table.

"You've been dating her for a while. Or at least a while for you. You usually love 'em and leave 'em pretty quickly." Ben chuckled, thinking back on all of the dates with different women his father had gone on in the last two years.

Max nodded thoughtfully. "Guess it has been a while."

"So. . . ."

Max slurped loudly. "So what?"

"Is she the one? Am I going to be calling Myrtle the Turtle Mom?"

Max lifted his gaze from the paper and Ben saw a bittersweet sadness in his father's gray eyes he'd not seen in a long time. "She's not the one," he said quietly.

"No?"

Max shook his head slowly. "She's not the one because there isn't going to be one. I guess I figured that out finally. Your mother was the one." His eyes glimmered with tears as he met his son's gaze. "My one and only."

"Ah, Pop," Ben said. Suddenly his father looked very small to him, very fragile. Old.

"I told Myrtle tonight that I'd be happy to keep escorting her here and there." Max glanced at the paper, taking control of his emotions. "I explained to her that I enjoyed her companionship, but I told her there wasn't any fire between us, not like I had with your mother."

Ben's heart twisted in his chest as his thoughts drifted from his parents' happy marriage to thoughts of Mackenzie. They had the fire, too, he knew they did.

"So," Max said. "I guess the search is over. I had a good marriage that lasted forty years. I got more than most men do, certainly more than I deserved."

Now Ben's eyes were tearing up. Partly for his father's loss and sadness, partly for his own.

"So I want to tell you, son. Whatever problem you've got with Mackenzie, you have to fix it. You have to make it right. Every man deserves one true love and she's upstairs right now." He glanced at his paper again. "That's all I'm going to say on the matter. I'm not going to stick my nose in again."

Thinking about what his dad said, Ben let the dog in. Passing through the kitchen, he drew his hand across his father's back. "Thanks, Pop," he said quietly.

"Welcome, son," Max said.

Ben went up to bed to try and get some sleep and figure out how he was going to get back on track with Mackenzie.

The next evening, Mackenzie reached Westview just in time to switch *Wheel of Fortune* on for her grandmother. She sat down in the chair next to the hospital bed and took the old woman's hand in hers. "Hey, sweetie," she said, patting the fragile, withered hand. "How are you tonight?"

She paused and waited, as if she was having a conversation with her grandmother. "Me?" she sighed. "Not great. Ben and I had our first real fight yesterday. It kind of went on all day, culminating with the man-walking-out-of-the-room scenario."

She slid her grandmother's hand under the light blanket and leaned back in the chair. "I remember what you said about never going to bed mad. I apologized. He said he was sorry about walking out, but that still didn't do it. This morning we both acted like we were fine, but we weren't."

She stared at her work boots that were splattered with paint. "Then he didn't call me all day. He always calls at work, just to say hi." She lifted one shoulder. "I know, he was probably just busy. Their business is really taking off but. . . ." She didn't bother to finish her sentence.

On the TV, Vanna was turning the letters. The answer was "tongue twisters" but so far, the contestants either hadn't figured it out or were taking their chances and trying to run up their cash.

"You know, Nana," Mackenzie said. "I really love him. I really do, but I'm wondering. . . ." She sniffed. "I'm beginning to wonder if he loves me. I mean *really* loves me."

She paused. "Why?" It was almost as if her grandmother was communicating telepathically with her. She could feel Nana listening, even if the older woman didn't appear to be following the conversation.

"I don't know . . . I . . ." She turned toward the

bed. "Do you think I would have been able to start this business if it hadn't been for my looks?" She leaned closer. "I mean, do you think these contractors are hiring me because my crews do a good job, or do you think they're hiring me because they want to meet me, be seen with me?" She frowned. "Check out my butt as I walk away after closing the deal."

She glanced back at the TV. Commercial break. There was a new floor wax out that shined and disinfected. Mackenzie wondered who ate off their floor.

Nana never answered Mackenzie, of course, but somehow, just being able to tell her, made Mackenie feel better.

Just as *Wheel* was ending, Mackenzie heard a knock on the open door.

"Mind if I come in?"

Mackenzie turned around in surprise. It was Ben! She didn't know what he was doing here; he'd never come on his own before. But she was tickled to see him just the same.

"Sure, come on in." She rose awkwardly from the chair. "Nana and I have been watching *Wheel of Fortune.*" She turned toward the bed. "Haven't we, Nana?"

"Hello, Mrs. Sayer," Ben said, coming to her bedside and taking her hand. "How are you tonight?"

As Mackenzie watched Ben look at her grandmother and speak so gently and kindly to her, a lump rose in her throat. Ben Gordon was a good man. The best. Watching him Mackenzie knew she had to figure out a way to get through this rough patch they were experiencing and make this marriage work. She knew in her heart that she could only truly be happy loving this man, having him love her.

"So what are you doing here?" Mackenzie asked Ben, touching him tentatively on his coat sleeve.

"I was in the neighborhood and thought I'd stop by. Thought you might want to stop somewhere and get something to eat—when you're done, here, of course." He slipped his hands in his coat pockets. "I don't want to hurry you along or anything."

Mackenzie glanced at her grandmother. "Actually I was about ready to go. Nana looks tired tonight."

"So, dinner?" he asked, obviously feeling as if he was treading on thin ice with her.

Mackenzie smiled, making him smile. "Just give me a chance to check in with the nurses' station and I'll be ready to go."

Eighteen

They took separate cars to the little pub on the edge of town and met in the parking lot. Ben wrapped his arm around his wife's waist as they walked inside and requested a table for two. The hostess escorted them to a snug alcove near the crackling fireplace and gave them menus. The restaurant was cozy and dark and smelled of wood planks and Irish ale.

"Feel like wine?" Ben asked, glancing over the menu. He didn't know why he was studying the pictures of half-pound cheeseburgers and fries so intently. He always ordered the blackened chicken salad. It was tasty and filling and it didn't run his cholesterol level up like those hunks of burger and mountains of fries.

"Wine might be nice."

Mackenzie smiled over the edge of her menu, making Ben think that perhaps he wasn't in as much trouble as he thought he was. Maybe his original suspicions were right. Maybe they were just getting though an initial adjustment period. If the problem Mackenzie had with him was a toothpaste cap and late trips to the supermarket, he could certainly make those changes in his life for her.

"Bottle or a glass?" he asked.

"Just a glass." She perused her menu.

When the waiter came, Ben ordered a zinfandel.

"I'll be right back to take your order in a minute," the young man said.

Mackenzie set down her menu to look at Ben across the table. "So how was your day?" she asked.

"Not bad. The addition on Chestnut is coming right along. And that Mr. Carol we had dinner with called. He wants to meet me at the houses next week to talk about definite plans." He sipped his water. "How about you? How did yours go?"

"Okay." She unfolded her napkin and placed it on her lap. "I hired another painter today and he does *not* drink."

They both laughed.

"And two big checks came in, so I can pay all of my bills." She pressed her hands to the table, her wedding band sparkling. "More money came in than went out, so I guess it was a good day."

"Sounds like a great day to me," Ben said, smiling. He knew what it was like to feel the pressure of a stack of bills on the desk, waiting for payment.

The waiter brought them each a glass of wine and then pulled out a pad of paper and a pen from his apron. "And what can I get you, folks?" He turned to Mackenzie to take her order first.

"I'll have the bleu cheese quarter-pounder, cooked medium-well, steak fries and steamed broccoli," she said.

The waiter nodded as if he approved.

Ben stared at his wife across the table and chuckled as he turned to the waiter. "While my wife is having the fifty-percent fat entrée, I'm going to have blackened chicken salad and the low-cal dressing. I guess calories aren't the same thing to her," he joked. "She'll probably want the cheesecake, too."

"Your order will be up shortly," the waiter said, headed for the swinging doors of the kitchen.

Mackenzie picked up her backpack and coat, and rose from her chair.

"You taking your coat to the ladies' room?" he asked, still amused by the thought that his wife could eat cheeseburgers while he had been relegated to grilled chicken years ago.

"No," she said, her voice beyond chilly, nearing frigid. "I'm taking my coat *home*."

In the time it took for what Mackenzie said to sink in, she stalked off. Ben just sat there for a moment in a daze. Now what did he do wrong? He got up and grabbed his coat to go after her, then realized he had to pay for the wine, and the dinner they had ordered for that matter. He tried frantically to catch his waiter's attention as he watched the restaurant door swing shut and Mackenzie walk out into the street.

The waiter returned to the table. "Yes, sir, is there a problem?"

Ben pulled on his coat and fumbled for his wallet. "Um, my wife—" He motioned to the door. "She's not feeling well."

"You want your meals to go?"

Ben glanced at the door again. He saw headlights in the parking lot. She was pulling out in her Porche. "No. No, just let me pay." He pulled a fifty from his wallet, watching as Mackenzie drove down the street past the restaurant windows. "Will that cover it and take care of your tip?"

"Yes, sir," the waiter said enthusiastically, stepping out of the way to let Ben pass.

Ben hurried out of the restaurant and across the parking lot. What was going on here? What had he said wrong now? He had tried to be understanding with Mackenzie, but finally he was losing his patience. No, he had *lost* his patience, he thought as he wheeled out of the parking lot and headed for home. He didn't know what was bothering Mackenzie or what he had done this time, or any of the other times, but they were going to have a talk. He was not going to live like this.

He loved Mackenzie, but he was not going to tolerate this kind of behavior. It was unfair to him and it was unfair to their relationship.

Mackenzie's car was in the driveway when Ben pulled in. He marched into the house. "Mackenzie!" She didn't answer, but the lights were on upstairs. She had to be in their bedroom.

Max came out of the kitchen.

"Mackenzie?" Ben asked his dad.

Max pointed upstairs.

The men's gazes met. Ben knew what his dad was saying without having to say it. *If you love her, go after her. If you love her, make it right.*

Without taking the time to remove his coat, Ben climbed the stairs, taking the steps two at a time. He walked into their bedroom to find Mackenzie packing a suitcase. She was still wearing her coat.

"What are you doing?" he exploded.

"What's it look like I'm doing?" she shouted back.

"I can see what you're doing. The question is why." He pulled a pair of jeans out of her hand and threw them on the bed. She grabbed them up again and threw them harder into her suitcase.

Howie stood between them looking back and forth in obvious doggy confusion.

"I'm leaving," she said, crossing the room toward her dresser. She grabbed an armload of socks, bras, and panties from the top drawer.

"What do mean you're leaving?"

"This isn't going to work." She shook her head, refusing to meet his gaze as she dumped the armful of undergarments into the suitcase. He could tell that she'd been crying. Her eyes were red and her cheeks were puffy. Her hair hung in her face, practically obscuring it. "We tried but it just isn't going to work."

"What won't work? I don't even know why you're angry with me."

"It doesn't matter." She slammed the suitcase shut, a sock dangling from one side, and heaved the load off the bed. The suitcase was obviously heavy, but no match for Mackenzie when she was angry.

"What do you mean it doesn't matter? Our marriage doesn't matter? The commitment we made to each other doesn't matter?"

"It's not your fault. It's my fault." She hurried out the door.

Ben stood there for a minute, collecting his thoughts, gaining control of his emotions. He heard her stomp down the steps.

Ben was so angry. So hurt. He had half a mind to just let her go . . . just let her go now, cool off, and then he'd track her down later. When they'd both had time to think.

But as he stared at the bedroom, her shoes in the open closet, a single rose in a vase on the nightstand, the smell of her perfume still in the air, he realized he didn't want to let her go, not even for a minute. He wasn't going to let her do this to him, to them. He'd waited too long for her to come into his life.

Ben ran down the stairs. "Going out, Pop!" he called as he ran past the kitchen door.

He saw Max at the sink, coffee cup in hand. "Don't come back without her," he warned.

By the time Ben got to the driveway, Mackenzie had already thrown her suitcase into the miniscule trunk and was climbing into the driver's seat of her old Porche. Ben caught the door before she slammed it in his face. He pushed his way into the car. "Move over."

Mackenzie stared in shock. Ben wasn't really being rough with her, but she was still surprised by his forcefulness. "What? No!" She pushed his shoulder.

"Move over, Mackenzie," he said firmly. "Move over or I'll move you over."

"What do you think you're doing?" she demanded as he nudged her into the passenger's seat. All she knew was that she needed to get away now before everything fell apart. That scene in the restaurant was just the beginning. Soon he'd be watching every bite she took, guarding her slender figure as if she were some prize heifer.

"You want to go for a ride?" Ben asked as he

squeezed into her car and slammed the door shut. "Fine, we'll go for a ride."

Mackenzie legs were in the air and she was half in the passenger's seat, half in the tiny space between the two seats.

"Better buckle up," he said, as he started the engine.

"I'm getting out!" she threatened, tight-lipped. "I don't want to talk to you." I'm afraid to, she thought.

Ben threw the car into reverse on the icy driveway, turned it around behind his SUV, and headed out of the driveway. "You're not getting out," he ordered.

She was shocked by his behavior, by the forcefulness of his words. She'd never seen him like this.

"You're going to go for a ride with me," Ben said angrily, "and we're going to talk about this."

"I don't want to go for a ride with you." She was shouting at him, but she couldn't hide the pain in her voice. She was on the verge of tears again.

"You *do* want to go for a ride with me. You want to go for a ride with me because this way, neither of us can walk out on the other." He turned onto a main street and headed south.

Begrudgingly, Mackenzie wiggled into a better position in her seat and hooked on her safety belt. Obviously, he wasn't going to stop to let her out. Like it or not, she was stuck with him, at least for the time being. "The window's fogging," she snapped and reached out to flip on the defroster. Ben gripped the steering wheel as if he were about to race the Indy 500. "Tell me what just happened back at the restaurant."

She stared straight ahead. Didn't he understand that she didn't want to talk about it? That she couldn't. That had been the problem all this time. She couldn't talk about how she felt.

"Mackenzie, we've got a full tank. We can cut across the Bay Bridge and make it well through the mountains before we have to stop for gas again." He took a quick look at her.

The streetlights didn't do much to illuminate the inside of the car, but she could see enough of his face to tell he was hurting too. A sob rose in her throat. She didn't want to hurt Ben. She loved him. She just wanted to get away before everything fell apart.

Ben was watching her, too. To her surprise, he reached out and covered her hand with his. As angry as he was with her, he still wanted to touch her. She felt her throat constrict as she fought her tears.

"Mackenzie, please," he said gently. The anger was gone from his voice. Now he was just upset, confused.

A sob escaped her lips. "You don't understand. . . ."

He looked at her as if he wanted to take her into his arms, but of course he couldn't because he was driving.

Ben pulled over to the side of the road under a streetlight and shut off the engine. A dog barked behind a nearby house, but no one seemed to take notice of them. Mackenzie stared straight ahead through the windshield into the dark night.

"No, I don't understand," he said. "Make me understand what's going on here." He unhooked his seat belt and moved as close as he could to her with the gearshift between. "Tell me," he murmured.

The yellow light of the street lamp seeped through her window, illuminating the handsome cheekbones and strong forehead of his face. Her hand shook in his as he waited.

"What did I say to upset you in the restaurant?" he pushed.

She didn't want to tell him. He wouldn't understand. She wasn't even sure she understood anymore. She was an adult, not the insecure, overly sensitive girl he'd known in high school. At least she'd thought so until recently. But from the day they'd married, the old fears and insecurities had haunted her, coming back more strongly with every word he said, every joke he made. It shouldn't be like this. She shouldn't be like this, but she couldn't seem to stop herself.

She'd been afraid for two months and she couldn't stand it any longer.

And he was being so sweet. He acted as if he wanted to understand. She sniffed, thinking about what her grandmother had once told her about taking risks. Nana had said that the greatest risks always resulted in the greatest joys. "My . . . my hamburger."

He blinked in confusion, but seemed to know better than to make a smart comment. "Go on."

"You said something about my hamburger while you were eating salad, as if I was going to get fat if I ate the burger." She let the words tumble out before she lost her nerve. "You even joked about my eating cheesecake." Now she couldn't stop the words. "I can't live my life worrying what you'll think about what I eat. Worrying about you worrying about me getting fat again."

"Whoa!" he said his face lined with confusion. "You're hitting me out of left field." He held her hand tightly. "I don't know what you're talking about, Mackenzie. I was commenting on the fact that my waistline and my cholesterol level can't stand cheeseburgers anymore. I wasn't commenting on your weight."

She tried to read his face. He looked sincere; he sounded sincere. Could she really have been this far off base? "But you comment about my looks all the time," she said, her voice barely audible.

He squeezed her hand. "I thought you liked compliments. Everyone likes compliments, Mackenzie."

"But not if that's all I am to you." Her last word came out as a miserable sob. It sounded ridiculous saying it, but that was how she felt. "A face and a body. I can't live up to that. No one can."

"Oh, sweetheart." He reached out and awkwardly tried to hug her in the tight confines of the sports car. "How can you say that? Of course that's not all you are to me."

"But the red dress. . . ." She sniffed. "The dinners with your clients, the 'This is my beautiful wife, Mackenzie' introductions." She tried to steady her voice. "It's all about what I look like, not about who I am."

"I'm sorry," he said, his voice heavy with emotion. "I didn't know you felt that way. It was never what I ever intended."

He stroked her back through her leather coat, and she breathed in the scent of his hair. She felt calmer now, more in control of herself.

"You should have told me you were sensitive about your looks," Ben said.

"It's just that once a fat girl, always a fat girl." There. She'd said it.

"Mackenzie." He took her chin between his finger and thumb and made her look into his eyes. Hers were full of tears. "It's time to let that go. That cannot be your definition of self."

Her lower lip trembled. He was right. She knew he was right. Just hearing the words aloud made her realize how right he was and how wrong she'd been all these years.

"So was that what the prom question was about?" he asked.

She nodded tentatively, starting to feel silly. What an immature reaction to her own insecurities. Ben was right; it was time to let all this go. How sweet he was to be so understanding, so tolerant of her lousy behavior.

He stroked her cheek. "Ah, honey. I didn't accept your invitation to the prom because I already had a date. Not because you were fat." He wasn't making light of her fears; he was being sincere.

She looked into his eyes and she believed him. Another lump rose in her throat, but this one was of happiness.

"I love you for who you are inside." He wiped at her tears. "For your sense of humor, for your girl-with-an-attitude style, for your brains, for the

way you treat my dad and your grandmother. I
love you for a million reasons and, frankly, your
cute ass is not at the top of my top one hundred
list."

She couldn't resist a laugh.

"Mackenzie, I'm sorry about all of this. But you
should have told me weeks ago instead of letting it
fester."

She hung her head but wouldn't allow herself to
feel guilty. A learning experience. These kinds of
things should always be learning experiences. "I
know. I just didn't know how to say it. I felt silly
and I suppose I was afraid there was truth to my
fears."

He stroked her head, smoothing her hair. His
touch made her feel so cherished, loved.

"If you think counseling would be a good idea,
I'll go," he offered.

She exhaled slowly, looking into his eyes. "That's
sweet. But honestly, I don't know that we need it.
Just finally telling you these things has made me
feel so much better."

Smiling, he leaned forward and kissed her. "I
love you," he said.

"Say it again," she whispered against his mouth.
Her heart was pounding, pounding with joy. Everything really was going to be all right.

"I love you." He brushed his lips to hers.

"Again."

"I love you, I love you, I love you, Mackenzie
Sayer Gordon. Fat, tall, skinny, short, ugly, or bald,
I'll love you forever."

She hugged him tightly and then gave him a
little push. "Let's go back to the house. I'm sud-

denly feeling as if it's bedtime," she said in a silky voice.

"Whatever you say, wife."

And they laughed together as Ben turned the car around and they headed for home.

Epilogue

Ten Years Later

"How are the clams coming?" Mackenzie called to Ben as she carried a cooler of drinks over the beach to the blankets spread out in the sand.

Ben glanced up from the clam pit and grinned. "I think they're ready."

Setting down the cooler, Mackenzie walked to the sandpit where the coals glowed and Ben eased his arm around her waist. It was growing dark, and the sun was setting over the bay in a brilliant ball of fading gases. He could hear the children laughing in the distance and the sound of Kayla's voice as she tried to herd them down the beach.

"Guess I should call everyone to eat, then. They've been complaining they were hungry for the last hour."

Ben pulled her against him, hip-to-hip, and kissed her. It was funny, but as the years passed, as they made their way through the landmarks of marriage, death, birth, hard times, and good times, Mackenzie's kisses became sweeter to Ben. More treasured.

"Where's Cody, hon?" Ben asked. Cody was their

five-year-old son and notorious for wandering off on one adventure or another.

"With his Uncle Zack, fishing with a pole and no line. Zack said he'd keep a good eye on him."

They laughed at the antics of their son and Ben felt his heart swell. He had never thought he would ever be a father, never thought he would enjoy fatherhood as much as he did. And he owed it all to Mackenzie.

"What's going on here?" Max called, coming over the sandy hill from where the cars had been parked. He was carrying a beach chair, wearing a floppy straw hat. "What's an old man got to do around here to get something to eat?"

Reluctantly releasing her, Ben grabbed a shovel and began to scoop up the ashes and coals from the pit. "Dinner's ready, Pop, if you want to round up the munchkins."

Just then, Abby came over the sand dune carrying another cooler with more food. Her nine-year-old daughter was right behind them, a bundle of towels in her arms.

Max walked to the edge of the shore, cupped his hands around his mouth and shouted, "Suppertime!" His voice was surprisingly loud and clear for a man his age.

As Ben dug the hot, steamed clams from the pit and placed them in a metal pan, Owen, Kayla, and Zack came up the beach, a trail of children behind them. Cody and Jason, Owen and Abby's son who was the same age as Cody, were dragging sticks through the sand. Savannah carried her six-year-old sister, Alison, piggyback.

"Dinner!"

"Can we have a drink?"

"I don't like clams."

"Can we have hot dogs?"

All the children were talking at once, clambering for food as Mackenzie passed out plates and flatware and Abby dished out potato salad and fruit salad.

By the time the kids had eaten and gone down the beach with Max and Savannah to find hidden treasure, the sun had set. With the kids fed and content, Zack, Owen, and Ben were finally able to take a seat on the beach blankets with their wives.

"The clams were great, dude," Zack said, sipping juice from a thermos.

"Fine job," Kayla said with a wink, leaning against Zack. "But now I need a nap."

Abby laughed as she handed Owen a soda and took a seat beside him to pick at what was left on her plate.

Mackenzie set aside her plate, wiggled between Ben's legs, and leaned against his chest. He wrapped one arm around her waist. A small bonfire crackled between them and the bay, illuminating the blankets in soft flickering light.

"This is the life," Ben sighed. "We ought to get together like this more often."

Over the years, with the coming of marriage, a child, and the pressures of business and family, Ben had discovered he just didn't have as much time for his friends as he once had. The nice thing was that though they didn't eat together or watch ball games on TV as often as they used to, things were always the same when they did get together. And it was funny, but instead of taking away from the relationships the guys had, Ben observed that the wives had added to it. Ben could honestly say that the love he shared with Mackenzie made him a better friend to Zack and Owen. And if the men were ever inclined to discuss the matter, he knew they would agree. And there was nothing like seeing his son play with one of Zack's or Owen's children. Ben, Owen and Zack's friendship had become a family tradition, now passing to a new generation.

"I say we give up our jobs and the house, and just live here on the beach," Mackenzie said dreamily.

Ben gave her a squeeze. "Wouldn't be much privacy," he teased in her ear.

Mackenzie laughed. "We could set up a tent, take turns using it?"

Everyone laughed.

Feeling nostalgic, Ben lifted his soda can high. "I think an evening like this calls for a toast."

Everyone reached for his or her cans, Zack for his juice thermos.

"A toast to friendship," Ben said, surprised by the emotion in his voice. "To love." He gave Mackenzie a squeeze. "And to the successful demise of Bachelors Inc."

"Hear, hear," everyone called as their soda cans clinked.

And as Ben lifted his drink to his lips, his gaze met Mackenzie's. "I love you," he mouthed.

"Say it again," she whispered.

"I love you, I love you, I love you," He squeezed her in a bear hug and they both fell onto the sand, laughing as only two people who found love later in life can.

ABOUT THE AUTHOR

Colleen Faulkner lives with her family in Delaware and is the author of twenty Zebra historical romances and four contemporaries. Colleen loves hearing from readers and you may write to her c/o Zebra Books. Please include a self-addressed stamped envelope if you wish a reply.

BOOK YOUR PLACE ON OUR WEBSITE
AND MAKE THE
READING CONNECTION!

We've created a customized website just for our very special readers, where you can get the inside scoop on everything that's going on with Zebra, Pinnacle and Kensington books.

When you come online, you'll have the exciting opportunity to:

- View covers of upcoming books

- Read sample chapters

- Learn about our future publishing schedule (listed by publication month *and author*)

- Find out when your favorite authors will be visiting a city near you

- Search for and order backlist books from our online catalog

- Check out author bios and background information

- Send e-mail to your favorite authors

- Meet the Kensington staff online

- Join us in weekly chats with authors, readers and other guests

- Get writing guidelines

- AND MUCH MORE!

Visit our website at
http://www.zebrabooks.com

Put a Little Romance in Your Life With
Fern Michaels

__Dear Emily	0-8217-5676-1	$6.99US/$8.50CAN
__Sara's Song	0-8217-5856-X	$6.99US/$8.50CAN
__Wish List	0-8217-5228-6	$6.99US/$7.99CAN
__Vegas Rich	0-8217-5594-3	$6.99US/$8.50CAN
__Vegas Heat	0-8217-5758-X	$6.99US/$8.50CAN
__Vegas Sunrise	1-55817-5983-3	$6.99US/$8.50CAN
__Whitefire	0-8217-5638-9	$6.99US/$8.50CAN